MAGICAL CREATURES ACADEMY

NIGHT SHIFTER

LUCÍA ASHTA

NIGHT SHIFTER

Magical Creatures Academy: Book One

LUCÍA ASHTA

For James,
my fiery lion

NIGHT SHIFTER

᪥ I ᪥

EVERY LIGHT IN THE LIVING ROOM WAS ON, REVEALING the droopiness of the well-worn furniture. The grandfather clock on the far wall creaked loudly with each sweep of its pendulum as it prepared to chime three times. My father and brother shared a nervous look with each other before pretending they hadn't—for my sake. So much of what they'd done the last few days had been to calm my nerves.

They'd failed miserably.

"Take a seat, Rina. You're not helping things by wearing a path into the hardwood floor," Dad said.

I met his eyes, always heavy, and then continued my pacing. It wasn't often that I dared disobey him so blatantly, but I'd earned this one. I couldn't stay still.

"Rina," Dad said, but the clock's hands clicked into place and the clock clanged three times. *Dumm, dumm, dummmm.* I'd always enjoyed the deep toll that was quintessential *home.* Tonight, it grated on my last nerve; one of my eyelids twitched.

Now that it was three in the morning, there was no way I'd be able to take a seat. Dad seemed to accept the fact, rubbing a hand across his tired face.

Three minutes. There were only three minutes left until my fate would be decided for me, and I wouldn't have a lick of a say as to how things would go down.

I chewed at my cuticles and picked up the pace.

"It's going to be okay," my brother said from his spot on the couch, the one that sagged from so many nights spent together when we'd tried to act as if we were a normal family.

I offered Ky a grimace. "Since when do you do empty platitudes?"

Under any other circumstances he might have smiled. "Since you won't stop moving. You're driving us nuts."

"Yeah, well, you're just going to have to deal with it. My entire life is about to be determined in a minute and a half."

No one said anything while a half-minute ticked by. Never had the grandfather clock's movements been so abrasive.

"Either way, it's going to be fine," Dad said. "Either you'll be a shifter like your brother"—and like my mother, though Dad rarely mentioned her unless he had to—"or you'll be a mage like me."

I snapped my head around to glare at him. "Or I'll be human. Did you just forget about that possibility?"

Dad cleared his throat and cast a fast look at the clock's hands. "It's incredibly unlikely that you'll be human when neither of your parents is, uh, was, ah..."

He cleared his throat again and I regretted my attitude for a moment.

My face softened, until I too glanced at the clock. "Thirty seconds." I swallowed loudly enough to be heard across the living room. Never had my throat been this dry.

I snapped my fingers from my mouth, clenched them together, and turned to face the clock as if it were a judge about to sentence me to life in prison.

Dad and Ky both opened their mouths—to say something soothing, I suppose—but in the end they said nothing and faced the clock. Ky stood and moved to my side; he draped an arm around my shoulders as if he did it every day, but I could tell he was as uncomfortable as I was. We hadn't touched on purpose since I started fifth grade and decided I was a big girl.

Even then I'd believed I was ready to grow up. How wrong I'd been. I'd give anything to have an extension and prolong my eighteenth birthday for at least another year. Once that minute hand circled to twelve, there was no going back, one way or another.

"Twenty-two seconds," I whispered as a wave of heat flashed across my skin. My birthday marked the beginning of winter, and yet I wanted to strip down to my tank-top. My cheeks flushed and Ky squeezed my shoulder. I didn't think he even realized he was doing it.

"Ten seconds," he said, and I ceased breathing entirely.

Dad rose from the couch and moved to my other side. He placed a hand on my forearm, but the touch was weak, as if he were as much a ghost as the mother who'd died birthing me.

"One second." My voice shook and tears pricked at my eyes. The temperature in the living room dropped by twenty degrees and I began to shiver. I turned eighteen.

Ky squeezed my shoulder so tightly that the tension I carried in my neck released under his touch. Dad removed his hand from me, crossed his arms, and turned to stare at me. "Do you feel anything? And … happy birthday."

I shook my head. My pulse whooshed loudly through my head and my palms had begun to sweat even as I trembled, but I felt like the same Rina I'd always been—awkward and unsure in my skin.

Ky stepped back to watch me too. For an entire minute I acted as if their joint stares didn't unnerve me. Then I snapped. "Take a picture, why don't you?" At the last moment, I turned toward Ky so Dad wouldn't think I'd said it to him too, though I had.

"Knock it off, you two," Dad said preventatively.

"I didn't even say anything," Ky protested.

"Yeah, but you were about to."

"I was not."

Ordinarily, I would have loved to comment how he sounded five, not twenty, but my tongue was in knots along with the rest of me.

I scratched my scalp, wondering why it was so itchy, and then flung my hands against my sides with a loud *thwap* that cut through the thick air of the living room. Usually comfy despite its large size, it felt as sterile as a surgical suite.

"Something should've happened by now," I said, my voice a little squeaky. "Right? I'm eighteen. If I were a shifter or a witch, something should've already happened."

"Maybe, maybe not," Dad said, and I struggled not to roll my eyes for fear I'd roll them so far into my head they'd stay there. "It could take a bit for anything to show."

"It didn't with Ky."

"You're different from him."

That was the understatement of the year. He was half a foot taller than me, broad shouldered, and filled with enough confidence that I often wondered if he'd stolen mine.

I bit my lip. "It's supposed to happen at the precise moment you turn eighteen. That's what all the books say."

"Books aren't always right," Dad said, an irony considering he'd spent his adult life compiling the authoritative volume on supernatural creatures, aptly named *The Compendium of Supernatural Creatures*. "Your magic might be delayed for some reason we aren't aware of. It could show up later."

I moved away from both of them and stalked to the other side of the living room, where I could stare out the large picture windows at the thick trees that had always soothed me, and pretend my entire world wasn't crumbling while Dad theorized to excuse my oddness—worse, my lack of powers.

With my back facing them, I voiced my worst fear. "I don't have any powers. I'm not a shifter and I'm not a witch. I'll be going back to school after winter break."

There was no immediate response. Disappointment thrummed through my chest, though I realized there was nothing comforting they really could say. At least half the offspring of supernatural creatures carried on some form of their parents' magic. But the supernatural community was notorious for its prejudices, and most bred within their own kind.

Not our parents. Theirs had been a story of true love—or at least that's how Dad told it on those nights when the nostalgia was too much and he allowed himself to drink in an attempt to soothe his loss. When the parentage was split between races, the odds that the children would carry their parents' magic plummeted to a quarter or less. Through their love, they'd doomed me to living as a human in the supernatural world—the only one I was familiar with.

Sure, I attended Berry Bramble High, where few were aware of the magical creatures that shared the world with them, but I'd never truly been one of the humans. I hadn't wanted to be, and so I'd never really fit in despite my group of friends, who believed I was just another teenager.

"My friends will be excited I won't be 'moving' after all." I spoke the empty-feeling sarcasm toward the cold window pane. "It's no big deal," I said, and immediately wondered why I'd speak such a blatant lie.

Footsteps padded softly across the floor behind me. Even without the socks softening his footfalls, I knew it was Ky and not Dad. Despite his size, my brother moved with the agility of a mountain lion, even when he was in human form.

"Don't touch me," I whispered when I sensed him behind me. For once I didn't say it to fight with him. I said it because if he tried to comfort me I might break, and it was taking everything I had not to crumble.

"Rina, it'll be okay, I promise." His tone was soft and soothing, something I hadn't heard since hormones raged through him and changed him into a supernatural creature I had no chance at being. "We'll figure it out. Together."

I chortled without a speck of mirth. "Together? Really? We haven't done anything 'together' for years. And now that it's clear I'm not part of our world—*your* world—there's no chance at *together*."

He scoffed, and I heard Dad start across the living room toward me. "That's not true," Ky said, even though it was. "I'm not going to just abandon you because you're human now. Dad won't abandon you. We're still like we've always been."

My focus went right to the important part of his statement. *I'm human now.* "You're wrong," I said, uncaring how they received my next words. "We haven't behaved as a family for a long time. You and Dad have always treated me like I'm the one who killed Mom. Like I'm to blame for our screwed-up family."

Dad halted, but I didn't regret what I'd said,

though I realized it was certain to hurt him. Any reminder of Mom and her absence hurt him. But I'd lived under that shroud all my life.

Ky reached for me, but I shook him off. "No. You know it's true."

"It's not."

"It is, and there's no point denying it. Mom died because of me—"

"Your mother died because she was hemorrhaging after she gave birth to you," Dad said, his voice nearly as silent as the deep night just beyond the window. "*I'm* the one who should have noticed what was happening to her. *I'm* the one that could have saved her and didn't. *I* am the only one to blame for her death and for the fact that you've had to grow up without a mother."

"Dad..." I said, ready to apologize for my selfishness. But he wouldn't let me.

"I raised you the best I could, but it hasn't been enough, and I realize that. But I will *not* abandon you just because you're human. If you won't be going to the Menagerie, then you'll stay here with me. You can help me with my work and contribute to the supernatural community that way."

Great. Just dandy. My life had gone from the possibility of going to study at the most prestigious school for supernatural creatures in the world to staying home with Dad and burying my nose in books that no longer had a thing to do with me.

"It will be great, really great." But Dad's voice was as empty as my chest, which felt like a big, pitch-black, empty cave where hopes withered and died.

"Sounds awesome, Dad," I said.

"Rina…" Ky tried again.

"It's late. I'm really tired. We should all get some sleep. No point burning the midnight oil anymore." I laughed, but it sounded more like a death rattle, spiraling hollowly around my throat. I cleared it just as Ky reached for me again.

I turned my face away so he wouldn't see my eyes shining with unshed tears and backpedaled rapidly. I bumped into Dad, sidestepped him without looking, and aimed for the hallway that led to my bedroom. My bare feet squeaked against the teak floor.

Ky and Dad called after me, but I took off in a run. The tears were coming, and after the crappy night I'd already had, I wasn't about to break down in front of them.

I reached the safety of my room when a barely audible knock sounded on the front door. My hand stilled on the doorknob while my heart beat so fast that I found it difficult to breathe.

I didn't dare turn. I didn't move at all while I worked to tamp down the hope that leapt to life inside me.

It was probably just a friend stopping by to wish me happy birthday. I hadn't been able to keep the dreaded 3:03AM birth time from my friends, since little more had been on my mind for the last month. We were on vacation. One of them might be up and swinging by, knocking timidly in case we were asleep.

Yeah, right, Rina. Then, without my permission, I dared to hope: It might be the Menagerie, coming for you just as they came for Ky.

No, if I'd been a shifter, I should have shifted shortly after my birth time. And if I were a witch, my magic would have flared.

I was human, human, human ... and so the Menagerie had no use for me.

My heart thudded erratically as I listened to Ky pad over to the door and swing it open.

❧ 2 ❧

"NESSA!" KY EXCLAIMED. "WHAT ARE YOU DOING here?"

"I'm here for your sister. Rina, is it?" a tiny, tinkly voice said, drawing me toward the foyer like a magnet.

"Yeah, my sister's Rina, but ... well, she's human."

My brother's words cut straight to my heart, incising out the ridiculous hope I'd allowed myself with the precision of a surgeon.

A ringing laugh, which reminded me of wind chimes, wafted down the hallway, and I padded toward it more quickly.

"Oh no, she isn't human," Nessa said.

"Sorry, but she is. Her birth time passed"— Ky consulted the traitorous grandfather clock—"almost ten minutes ago. She's shown no signs of magic whatsoever."

I stilled at the end of the hall, from where I could make out our uninvited guest, as small as a humming-bird, and flitting at Ky's eye level much like one: a blue-haired fairy dressed in far too little clothing for the longest night of the year.

"Hunh," the fairy was saying. "That's odd, now isn't? Sir Lancelot himself ordered me here to invite her to join the Menagerie."

I was pretty sure Ky said something in reply, but I didn't register it. The blood rushed to my head, or maybe it was more accurate to say that it rushed from it. The thumping, marching band had resumed residence in my cranium, and my eyeballs and lips were beginning to feel numb. My heart bounced around in my chest like I was a racquetball court. Eighteen was too young to have a heart attack, right?

"Is that her?" Nessa said, drawing my attention to her as I slumped against the wall.

Dad rushed to my side, but stopped short of touching me. "Are you ... okay?" He peered at me while I blinked rapidly, trying to bring his thick chestnut hair and matching eyes into focus.

When I didn't answer, he reached a tentative hand toward me. At his touch, I startled and jerked.

"Rina," he said, "I think you need to sit down."

I nodded stupidly and allowed the father who'd touched me maybe ten times in the last year to guide me over to an oversized leather armchair, where I sank into its depths without ceremony.

"Boy, she doesn't look to be doing so well," Nessa said, her voice sounding far away though she'd begun to move toward me once Ky ushered her in. Her wings moved so rapidly that they were little more than a blur, and in seconds she buzzed in front of me.

Under ordinary circumstances, I'd be annoyed at the invasion of my personal space. Of course, there was nothing ordinary about the situation.

"Is she … you know?" Nessa asked.

"No, we don't know," Dad snapped, and the edge to his voice began to lure me out of my haze. Dad rarely reacted strongly to anything.

The tiny woman, who could only be a fairy, brought both hands to her hips, akimbo, and studied me, seemingly unbothered by Dad's attitude. "I mean, is she all there?"

"Are you asking if she's mentally challenged or something?" Dad growled, and he sounded a bit like Ky when he got angry and his animal rose to the surface.

But Nessa nodded happily and smiled until I wondered if the fairy might be a bit mentally challenged herself. "That's exactly what I'm asking," she said. When Dad replied only with another growl—an honest-to-goodness growl—she finally moved her attention to Ky. "Well?"

Ky spoke through tight lips. "She's quite intelligent. She's just having a bit of a hard time adjusting, which is understandable. She hasn't shifted or sensed any magic. She believed she was human. We all did."

"Well, that's nonsense." The fairy, whose tiny skirt and top matched her bright hair, waved a hand in dismissal and drew nearer to me. I flinched and pulled my face back, but she only flew in closer. "She's obviously a shifter of some sort, or one of the other oddball supernatural creatures. Sir Lancelot wouldn't have sent me if it were otherwise." She nodded matter-of-factly, oblivious to the looks the three of us were giving her. "What? What'd I do?"

Dad shook his head repeatedly and opened his mouth to reply before he noticed Ky giving him his own shake. Dad arched his eyebrows in question.

Ky ignored Nessa's question and said, "So you're sure Rina is a supernatural creature? Even if she hasn't displayed any powers and it's already well past the time when it's supposed to happen?"

"Of course I'm sure, silly. Isn't that what I just said? You know the spell that dictates which students get invited to the Menagerie doesn't make mistakes. And neither does Sir Lancelot."

"No, the owl wouldn't. I've never met a creature more concerned with precision." Ky rubbed at the stubble on his chin until his brandy eyes, exactly like mine, lit up. He grinned. "That means you've got magic, Rina. It must."

"Really?" My question was barely a whisper. "I don't feel any different, not even a little bit. Surely something would have changed in me. Anything."

"I don't understand it either, but Sir Lancelot wouldn't make a mistake like that."

"The spell that governs the Menagerie's student selection has been in place for over a hundred years." Dad, now in his element, sounded like a textbook. "It was set up by the school's founders, Mordecai and Albacus. They were some of the finest wizards of their time. Given that they lived for centuries, their knowledge is some of the most substantial of the magical world. If their spell selected you, then you must be a magical creature."

For once I didn't mind Dad droning on about magical history. "So there's no way this could be a mistake?"

"Girl, didn't you hear me?" Nessa said. "None. Not even a bit."

My heart started beating so that I noticed it again, racing happily. "You're sure?" The numbness in my lips and eyeballs remained, but I was pulling in deep, steady breaths now so I wouldn't pass out before I could celebrate. "You're one-hundred percent certain?"

Nessa faced Ky. "Are you sure she's all there? I did just explain..."

"She's all there, all right," Dad snapped again and took several menacing steps toward the tinkly fairy, who retreated toward me again. While Dad was as tall as Ky at six-foot-two, he wasn't nearly as brawny. But right then, with his eyes looking like they might bulge out of his skull, his fists clenched at his side, he appeared every bit as intimidating as Ky and his foot-ball linebacker body.

Nessa put up her hands and blinked tiny long lashes. "Whoa there. I'm just doing my job here. No need to get all snippy."

"You haven't seen snippy yet. Call her stupid one more time and you will."

"I didn't call her stupid." And the fairy actually sounded like she believed it. I, however, was more surprised by the fact that Dad and Ky were so intent on defending my honor—or intelligence or whatever.

I blinked rapidly to hide the tears as a swell of emotion overcame me.

"What's she crying about?" Nessa said. "Most people are excited when the Menagerie comes knocking. Not just anyone gets in. They have to be suited to the school, and that's determined by a whole bunch of factors I'm not privy to, but I know they're a lot."

The blue fairy zoomed back in front of my face, studying my eyes one by one as if to check for some unknown evidence of my acumen. "It's relatively uncommon for siblings to be accepted to the school, too, so you're extra lucky. There are only a few pairs of siblings in the entire student body at the moment. So the fact that Kylan was accepted actually minimized your chances. That your mother attended doesn't really have much of an impact, as admittance is reviewed on a case-by-case-basis."

"That's quite enough," Dad said, cutting off the fairy's rambling. "My daughter's extremely overwhelmed at the moment. Give her some space."

"Hunh. Fine." But the fairy only flew back half a foot and crossed her arms in front of her chest. "I don't have all night though." She tilted her chin upward. "I have plenty of very important responsibilities that Sir Lancelot is relying on me to complete. For the good of the school."

"I have no doubt," Dad said. "And we won't hold you up a second longer than necessary. If you're here to offer her entrance to the Menagerie, get on with it."

"I already did, now didn't I?" But Nessa turned a solemn look on me regardless. She cleared her throat importantly and crossed her hands behind her back as she hovered directly in my line of sight. "Rina Nelle Mont, you've been selected to attend the Magical Creatures Academy, also referred to as the Menagerie, where magical creatures of all kinds go to learn about their powers and how they can best contribute to the well-being of both supernaturals and humans alike."

I nodded as if in a dream.

"If you agree to attend the Academy, you'll be agreeing to the following: You'll at all times behave in a manner that's consistent with the mission and integrity of the school. You'll do your best to become the most powerful version of your creature that you can be. And upon completion of all necessary curriculums, you'll join the Menagerie Force tasked with ensuring that no shifter, vampire, or other supernatural creature within our purview harms another of our kind or a human."

The fairy puckered her lips and directed her gaze toward the ceiling. "Hmm, I think that's it. If I've forgotten anything, you'll have plenty of time to read up on the school before you show up for your first day."

I stared at her.

"Well?" she prompted. "Do you, Rina Nelle Mont, agree or not? I'm not allowed to give you your admittance papers until you verbally give your consent."

I chuckled. "Of course I agree!" Joining the Menagerie had been the one thing I'd allowed myself to dream of since I first learned that Mother had attended.

"I need your consent with your full name please." The fairy was all business now.

"Do I need to say something in particular, or just anything?"

"No, not *anything*. Your consent for me to extend your official invitation."

I rolled my eyes, but the fairy didn't seem to mind. "I, Rina Nelle Mont, give my consent for you to, er, extend my invitation to the Magical Creatures Academy."

"Good enough!" The fairy reached a hand toward her wings and emerged with a fairy-sized canister for a fairy-sized scroll that had been strapped to her back. She removed the cap from the canister with a *pop* and slid the scroll out. "Here, you'd better take it."

She shoved it at me so quickly that it tumbled into my lap. I was scrambling to retrieve the dime-sized scroll when it popped again and enlarged until it was human sized. "Wow. That's cool." I gaped at the rolled-up scroll.

"Yeah," Ky said with a true grin on his face, making his face look as handsome as all my friends claimed it to be. "You're gonna love it at school. Everything's cool there."

"It is pretty awesome, if I do say so myself," Nessa added, grinning as widely as my brother.

I shifted a concerned look at Dad, but he didn't seem to feel left out. He was back to looking aloof, as if he preferred the world of his books to the real one. I swallowed a heavy sigh.

"So am I supposed to sign or what?"

"You can now, or you can read over all the fine print and bring it with you on your first day."

"Nah, I'm ready to sign now." I struggled to keep my cool. My legs bounced and I was desperate to run around the house screaming like I was ten years younger.

"That's the way," Nessa said while reaching to her back again. She emerged with a diminutive pen that I wouldn't be able to use to sign if I tried. She tossed it to me as if we were in a game of hot potato and the timer was about to run out.

Again the item tumbled into my lap, but before I could do much searching for it, another pop transformed it into a sophisticated fountain pen that fit perfectly in the palm of my hand. I spread the scroll on the side table next to the armchair and looked at the fairy expectantly.

"Well?" she finally said. "What are you waiting for?"

"For ink," I enunciated carefully. I was pretty sure the fairy would give me a headache if we hung out for long.

She *tsked*. "You don't need ink. You have to sign in blood. Didn't the supposed authority on the magical community teach you anything?"

Dad didn't even react to her "supposed." His eyes were glazed and I wondered where he'd gone. Probably with Mom, when he'd last been happy.

While keeping a cautious eye on Dad, Nessa whispered, "Sir Lancelot is actually the authority on all things magical creatures, probably magical history too. There's no one smarter than he."

"Hey," Ky said, but his heart wasn't in his defense of Dad. He was glancing at him worriedly too.

This was my big moment. I forced my attention back where it belonged. "Do I just … poke my vein with the pen until I draw blood or what?"

"Oh no. We're not savages." And the fairy was back to considering me as if she'd never met anyone as dense. "But since there aren't any vamps around, feel free to press the nib to the vein in the crease of your elbow until blood pools there."

That sounded savage to me, but when Ky nodded his encouragement, I did just that. No sooner had I pressed the pen to the crook of my arm than crimson ink welled to the surface. Of course it was an enchanted pen, I should have known!

I removed the pen from my flesh when there was enough blood.

"Make sure you sign your full name," the fairy said.

I signed Rina Nelle Mont in big, flourishy letters that were quite unlike my usual script. When I swiped at the remaining blood on my arm with my other hand, there wasn't so much as a pinprick, just a few drops of smeared blood; the pen had taken exactly enough.

Nessa flew down to blow on the paper. When it

NIGHT SHIFTER

became obvious her small breath would take forever to dry anything, I joined in.

"Whoa, whoa, whoa. Back off! You about blew me across the room."

"Oh. Sorry." I grimaced. "I didn't realize."

"I noticed." The fairy scowled. "Leave the job to the professional, will you?"

"Sure, fine."

The fairy gave me a you-really-don't-know-what-the-hell-you're-doing look, then flew back down to the scroll, all the while training a wary eye on me. She blew for long enough that she grew tired and called it "good enough," then tapped the scroll to activate its inherent magic. The scroll popped back to fairy size and she snatched it up. Another tap shrank the pen, and she stowed them both in her shirt.

"School term resumes exactly two days after the New Year. I'll see you and Kylan in Sedona at 8 a.m. sharp. Rina, present yourself to the administration office."

I nodded like a bobblehead. "I'll be there. After the New Year. In Sedona. On time."

"Good. See that you are." The fairy offered Ky a nod, then, "Goodbye, Mister Mont."

"Oh," Dad said. "Goodbye, and thank you for coming all this way for Rina."

Nessa stared at Dad for a long while before finally saying, "You're welcome. Take care of yourself, Mister Mont."

Great. Even the fairy could tell our dad was half there, half somewhere else. He nodded absently as I rose to my feet, joining Ky in escorting Nessa to the door.

He swung it open and she flew out without further ado. The sound of jingling bells followed her out into the night, which was suddenly filled with enough joy to brighten its darkness.

Ky closed the door, but the next chapter of my life was only just beginning. It didn't make a lick of sense. I hadn't shifted, nor had I burst with magic, but I was a student at the Magical Creatures Academy.

Not even Dad's usual moroseness could dampen my mood. I beamed at Ky. He beamed right back.

3

"HERE WE ARE," DAD SAID AS HE PULLED OUR decade-old Land Rover to a stop in one of a half dozen available parking spaces.

I leaned forward in the back seat to check out a sign that announced we were at the trailhead to the Thunder Mountain Trail. "Uh, we're at the base of a mountain."

"Hm-hmm." Dad was already slipping the car keys into his pocket and opening his door.

"Wow," Ky said from the passenger seat. "I think I've missed this place. I wasn't sure I would after last term."

"Last term? What happened last term?" I asked.

"Oh, nothing. It was just a lot of work that's all."

I narrowed my eyes at Ky, who refused to meet my querying gaze, while Dad stepped out of the car with a groan. Ky pushed open his door.

"Wait, are you guys serious? Is this really the place?"

"Yep," Ky answered and stepped outside, stretching his back. "Man, that was a looong ride. I'm so relieved it's finally over. Next time we should definitely fly."

"Then I wouldn't be able to come with you," Dad said. "And this is Rina's first term. It's a big deal."

He didn't have to say that twice. My stomach had been churning since we'd crossed Kansas.

"But it won't be Rina's first term next time," Ky said. "And I'm worried about you driving all the way back on your own."

Dad clapped Ky on the back. "It's the parent's job to worry about the kids, not the other way around." He smiled, but it didn't quite reach his eyes. I think he realized that both Ky and I worried about him. Even though Dad kept to himself a lot, at least I had still been home to check up on him. With both Ky and I gone, I wasn't sure what would happen to Dad.

Ky caught my eyes. He was thinking the same thing. We hadn't talked about it, but then, we hadn't had to.

"I'm going to take my time driving back, make it an experience. Stop at all the popular tourist traps along the way and make a thing of it."

Dad hadn't made a thing of much of anything for as long as I could remember. When Ky and I were younger, he'd made more of an effort. Once we were old enough to more or less take care of ourselves, he'd retreated into his study more and more to work on his research.

"You'll text us along the way and let us know how your trip's going?" Ky said.

"If you want me to."

"Please," Ky said, before turning toward the very large and very solid mountain that looked absolutely nothing like a school for magical creatures. He smiled and zipped up his coat against the bitter wind whipping past.

I zipped my own jacket and joined them outside, pulling the small duffel bag I'd packed across my chest. Ky assured me that since the school required uniforms, I needed nothing more than underwear, pajamas, other personal items, a few lounge clothes, and a couple of informal outfits. I bent down to tie a shoelace that had come undone. Boy was I glad I still got to wear my Converse. I had them in enough colors to suit my every mood.

I craned my neck to take in the entirety of the mountain. From its base, it looked to be higher than six-thousand feet tall, but what did I know about mountains. We lived in the middle of Iowa's boonies, where everything was flat and covered either in corn or in snow, depending on the season.

"Are you guys sure you're not yanking my chain? How can this be a school?"

"I knew you'd never read my books," Dad said, and for the first time ever I actually wished that I had.

"Dad, your books are basically encyclopedias. No one reads encyclopedias."

But he refused to meet my eyes. "It doesn't matter. It's just my life's work. Who cares?"

"Dad…" I inched toward him, unsure what to do. Our family didn't do hugs. "I promise I'll read them when I get home." I only made promises I intended to keep, which made me already dread the seven thick books of his *Compendium* I'd have to wade through.

"Don't bother," he said, but he didn't sound bitter as I expected he would. "You're going to learn all you need to learn here." His voice was suddenly peppy and it instantly made me suspicious. "And speaking of, you don't want to be late for your first day of school." He checked his watch. "It's almost seven."

Despite the early hour, I was wide awake. We'd arrived in Sedona late last night and slept in a local inn. The bed had been comfortable, the room quiet, but I'd tossed and turned most of the night. I should've been exhausted, but I could barely stand still.

"Come on, squirt," Ky said.

"You know I hate it when you call me that."

His grin said that he realized exactly how much it bothered me.

"Will you at least not call me that in front of every-one?" I said. "I'm nervous enough as it is, and I'm pretty sure I won't need your help embarrassing myself. I tend to do that well enough all on my own."

Ky patted me on the back a little too hard. "Don't worry so much, squirt. You'll do fine. You're going to love it here."

I narrowed my eyes at him and jutted out my chin in my most threatening look. It made him laugh. "Great!" I returned my face to normal and flung my hands in the air in exasperation. Another fierce gust of wind whipped my long blond hair across my face, sticking the tangled strands to my mouth and eyes. I rushed to sweep my hair away and tuck my face into the high collar of my jacket while bouncing on my feet. "If this is really the school, lead the way."

Ky's eyes twinkled before he turned to Dad. "Take care of yourself. We'll see you at the end of May, okay?"

"Of course, son. I'm only a phone call away if you need anything."

"Is Dad not walking us in?" I again took in Thunder Mountain. How on earth were we going to get "in" when it was solid rock?

"He can't," Ky said. "You can only enter if you're a supernatural creature, and even then, only if you've been invited."

"The spell provides some exceptions for mages the school needs for maintenance or teaching," Dad said. "But unless the school requires a magician, none of them are allowed in. It's all in my 'encyclopedias.'"

I grimaced and moved next to Dad. "All right, then, I guess. Uh, see you later, Dad? I'll miss you." I wasn't entirely sure how I felt about leaving him behind, but it seemed like the thing to say. I loved Dad and all. It's just that things were never easy with him.

He patted me on the back as he had Ky, though far more awkwardly. "Be careful," he said. "The school can be dangerous if you don't watch yourself."

"It can? You've never mentioned it before. Seems like the kind of thing someone should've mentioned."

Ky gave Dad a look, grabbed his own small duffel bag, slung it across his body, closed his car door, and draped an arm across my shoulders, making me instantly suspicious. "Let's go, squirt. You're going to be fiiiine. Besides, I can't take these crazy nerves of yours another second. Time to rip off the Band-Aid and get you in there."

I jerked my head back to look at him. "Rip off the Band-Aid? Is this going to hurt?"

"Not a bit." He gave me his best salesman smile.

"You're not telling me everything." I tried to snake out from under his grip, but he only pulled me more tightly against his side.

"Of course I'm not telling you everything. I've barely told you anything about the school at all."

That was true; he hadn't. I narrowed my eyes to thin slits.

"I didn't want to bore you with it all." I growled and he laughed. "You're going to be just dandy, I promise. Most students make it through the first term with all their limbs intact, so not to worry."

"*Most* students?" I squeaked.

"Ky," Dad admonished. "Don't mess with her."

I sighed in relief. "Thank goodness. For a second there I thought you were for real."

Suddenly Dad and Ky found the towering tan and reddish mountain fascinating.

"Ky," I warned.

"No time to dilly-dally," he said. "Bye, Dad. See you soon."

"Bye, guys. Good luck to both of you. Hope you don't need it—much."

And with that ominous farewell, Ky swept me along despite my attempt to drag my feet, and led me around the base of the mountain, the one that apparently housed an entire secret world within it.

DAD WAS GONE FROM SIGHT AND WE STILL HADN'T entered the mountain. "Are you sure you guys aren't messing with me?" I asked.

"Of course we aren't," Ky answered distractedly, though it was exactly the kind of thing he'd do. Maybe not Dad, but definitely Ky. "I always forget exactly where it is... Oh! There!"

I followed his gaze but saw nothing but mountain yet again. But now he was tugging on my arm and excitement quickened his steps. I couldn't help but respond with some hopeful anticipation of my own. If this was how Ky was responding, then the school must be as amazing as he claimed it was—all the while omitting a variety of details. Back home, that hadn't seemed as important as it did now, when I'd preferred to hang out with my friends over him.

He speed-walked ahead, making me skip a few steps to keep pace with his longer legs. At five-eight, I wasn't short, but those extra six inches he had on me added up quickly.

He was walking straight at the mass of mountain, which was drawing close, when I started pulling on his grip. He tightened his hold and kept pulling. "Not now, Rina," he said.

"But you're heading straight for the rock!"

He didn't respond in any way beyond tugging. Then he walked smack against the mountain...

And his entire body disappeared. All but the hand latched on to my arm.

He gave me one final, rough tug—that I was totally going to pay him back for later—and I tumbled face-first inside Thunder Mountain.

I let loose a startled little scream before fright shut me up. Never before had I been so grateful for my bullheaded big brother, who continued to grip my arm though I could no longer see him, not even the hand that gripped me. I couldn't even make out my *own* hand.

It was pitch black as my eyes adjusted from the morning sunshine of outside. We were clearly inside the mountain, so magic was obviously at play. Would it have killed them to light some flashlights or torches or whatever it was that magicians did?

When Ky tugged this time, I was only too happy to follow his lead. His pace had slowed, so I was able to shuffle along to ensure I didn't trip and fall flat on my face, where the mountain might swallow me up or something equally awful.

It seemed like we'd walked for ten minutes, though it was probably more like a minute since ten minutes would have placed us close to the middle of the mountain, when my next step felt different, and I placed it tenderly on the ground in front of me, which I still couldn't see.

Our walk so far was strange, and it went beyond the fact that Ky and I were walking in an inkwell in the middle of what had appeared to be solid rock. The air around us felt oddly artificial, as if I were breathing thinner-than-ordinary oxygen. Each step, though landing on firm ground, gave me the odd sensation that I was walking on air.

That sensation ended as my right foot descended on something different. I hurried to pull my other leg through and was rewarded with light bright enough to force me to squint.

Annnd there was the sun, creeping up the sky as the morning progressed. How on earth was there a sun inside a mountain? And how the hell were Ky and I in it?

I blinked rapidly as my eyes watered. When I could finally focus again, I pinned a glare on Ky that was quickly replaced by awe. He dropped his hand from my arm and I spun in place.

Wow.

We were in the middle of a bright forest, the kind I'd always imagined was home to the fae. The trees were huge, tall with thick canopies. The air was rich and clean, and I filled my lungs. Bright flowers in every shade lined the pebbled path we stood on, and butterflies, bees, and hummingbirds flitted about doing their pollination awesomeness.

The skies of Sedona were a shocking bright azure, and that one similarity continued inside, where the rest of it looked nothing like that arid desert with its rocky terrain the color of terracotta. The sound of running water sprang from somewhere, and a happy soft tinkling echoed that made me think of the laughter of fairies—the ones I imagined in my idyllic fae world and who were nothing like Nessa.

"Why didn't you tell me?" I whispered to Ky.

He grinned from ear to ear, the expression lighting up his entire face. "I didn't want to spoil it for you."

"I don't think there's any spoiling this." I turned in place again, trying to take it all in and failing. There were so many little details that varied from the outside world. I could probably spend an entire day exploring just this area and not register it all. Every one of my senses was stimulated to bursting with all the color, sound, and crisp scents.

"I'm still going to kill you for not warning me about the entry," I told Ky. "That was so not cool. I thought the mountain was going to swallow me up."

"What? And spoil all my fun?"

"I'm definitely going to kill you."

"Well, killing me will have to wait," he said. "We have to check in. The rabbit gets grumpier the later it gets, and trust me, you don't want him in a bad mood."

I didn't imagine that a grumpy bunny would be all that bad, but when Ky took off down the flower-lined path, I followed right away. My duffel bag bounced against my side as I picked up the pace to match my long-legged brother.

❧ 4 ❧

I HESITATED AS SOON AS THE RABBIT CAME INTO FOCUS, standing in front of a resplendent gate that towered over him, glittering in the early morning sunlight. The entrance was going for a Pearly Gates feel: unnecessarily large and majestic, dazzling with precious metals and gems. This was a school, not a palace. Granted, it was a school unlike any I'd ever seen, but the gate was over the top.

"Oh no you don't," Ky said, taking my arm. "Remember what I've taught you about predators?"

"You haven't taught me jack squat to prepare me for this." I dragged my feet, and when Ky wouldn't allow that, I at least managed to slow down a bit.

He scowled, but didn't bother denying that he'd explained far too little about the school. I hadn't realized it until now; he should have well before. "You never show weakness in front of predators," he said. "They thrive on it. You don't provoke them, for sure, but you also don't give them the impression they can push you around and eat you for lunch."

"He's just a rabbit." My voice shook.

"Tell yourself whatever you want to get through this. But that's not 'just a rabbit.' That's a predator, which is why he protects the entrance to the school. No one gets by him that isn't supposed to. Follow my lead."

I gulped and took in the entirety of the rabbit while he was distracted with another student. I couldn't hear what he was saying to the girl, who appeared to be my height and age, though it was always difficult to tell with magical creatures. With magic, things were rarely what they seemed.

The rabbit, standing on his hind legs, was as tall as Ky and nearly as solid. His fur and coloring were much like a cotton-tailed bunny's—and that's where the similarities ended. His jackrabbit ears stood tall and at attention, twitching and tilting to listen in all directions. Along with his black, pupil-less eyes, I doubted the rabbit missed a thing. But his teeth were the worst; they were sharp and pointy, and there were far too many of them. This rabbit didn't munch on leaves...

His beady eyes flicked to me and I froze in place until Ky pulled me along and I stumbled over my own feet. The rabbit smiled a vicious, wicked sneer.

"You should've told me," I whispered to my brother's back, certain the rabbit would hear if I spoke any louder.

When my brother didn't respond at all, I

wondered if the rabbit could hear farther than the thirty or so feet that separated us. I pursed my lips shut and was tempted to pray, and I hadn't even officially entered the school yet.

The rabbit wore black pants, which revealed a bulge where I'd hoped there wouldn't be one, and a button-down shirt—with the top button open but the shirttails tucked into his pants. His large rabbit feet were bare, revealing a set of sharp claws I wouldn't want to find myself on the end of.

He finished with the girl and directed his full attention to us. "Hurry it up, then," he said in a voice that matched a movie mobster's—cold, calculated, and deadly. "I don't have all day. You're running late as it is."

I didn't think we were actually running late. We were supposed to check in by eight, and it couldn't be half past seven.

"Sorry, Rasper," Ky said, and I had to catch my jaw before it dropped. Ky rarely said sorry, and he especially didn't apologize when there wasn't reason to.

"My sister's new," Ky continued, and I wanted to kick him. Rasper the Rabbit's eyes latched on to me. "You know how it is with new students. It's all overwhelming."

"Maybe, but that's not my problem." He motioned us forward with fluffy paws—with a matching set of vicious claws—and I nearly ran to obey his command.

He sneered at me again, and a chill set in that was worse than the harsh Sedona winter winds. "There's a line forming behind you when there shouldn't be. I run a tight operation. I don't do lines."

There were two students only just popping into sight behind us on the path. The rabbit would be finished with us long before they caught up.

"Sorry, Rasper," Ky said.

The rabbit *hmphed*. "Full names for the record."

"I'm Kylan Bond Mont, and this is my sister, Rina Nelle Mont."

"Each needs to speak his or her own name for the record."

Ky didn't even roll his eyes. My brother behaving so differently than his norm made me almost as nervous as the rabbit did.

"I'm Rina Nelle Mont," I said in little more than a whisper. Ky shot me a look that reminded me of his predator warning, but what did he expect me to do? He was lucky I hadn't gone running in the opposite direction despite the firm hold he continued to maintain on me.

The rabbit considered me for a long while, then nodded. His rigid ears didn't flop with the movement.

"Kylan Bond Mont, I'll need blood evidence."

Ky hesitated. "Come on, Rasper. You know me. This is my fourth term."

"Rules are rules, Mister Mont. They're made to ensure complete and absolute security of the Magical Creatures Academy. If I make an exception for you, disorder ensues." I was in the middle of thinking how ridiculous this was when the rabbit clearly knew my brother when he added, "I must verify that you are not an impostor. There are those that must be kept out at all costs, you know that as well as I. The supernatural community is in turmoil. The strictest security measures are a necessity if we are to survive."

Yeah, Ky didn't tell me jack squat about who needed to be kept out either. I should've read Dad's *Compendium*. I should've done *something* to better prepare. My pulse was looping through my body like a stampede of horses, and I wasn't even in danger—I didn't think.

"Of course," Ky said, and I turned to look at the acquiescing stranger who stood in the place of my brother. "Forgive me, Rasper. You're absolutely right." Ky slid out of his jacket and pushed up the sleeve of his shirt. "Here you go." He offered the crook of his arm to the rabbit, who nodded in approval.

Rasper wore a black leather utility belt around his waist, and from it he removed a tool that looked like a glass straw but couldn't be. He pressed it to Ky's arm and blood welled to meet the tip immediately. After securing a few drops, the rabbit lifted the device and the remaining blood seeped back into my brother's skin. He removed a device a bit like what would result if a pocket mirror and a compass had a baby, laid it flat in his open palm, and waited until its bells and whistles stilled entirely.

I leaned forward. The device had needles marking gauges just beneath the surface of the glass. The rabbit pressed the tip of the glass straw to the depression in the center of the device. The glass face sucked the blood beneath it.

Ky leaned over it to watch too as the entire contraption lit up. A wisp of blood fog circled around the thing in a frenzy while it whistled and rocked in the rabbit's hand like a kettle achieving boil. Just as I began to suspect that the compass-thingy might blow, it simmered, settled, and then emitted a single *dum-da-dum-dum-dum, dam-dam.*

The rabbit jerked his head in a single nod of approval. "Your blood matches that on file. Mr. Kylan Bond Mont, you may enter the Magical Creatures Academy." Rasper the Rabbit swung toward the pearly gates behind him.

"Rasper, would you be so kind as to allow me to accompany my sister inside?" Ky said in a totally unfamiliar placating tone. When the rabbit didn't respond, Ky added, "I'd love to inform her of the school's magnificent history as she first takes it in."

"Very well. I'll allow it this one time."

Never had I been so grateful for my brother's company as I slipped off my own jacket and extended my arm to the killer rabbit, who repeated the process exactly.

My blood took longer to achieve approval, but that could also be because every moment in such close proximity to the hare had my scalp tingling and my legs itching to run in the opposite direction.

Finally the rabbit said, "Miss Rina Nelle Mont, your blood matches that on file. You may enter the Magical Creatures Academy."

"Thank you," I squeaked, and hurried to put distance between the hare and me. I tucked my jacket through the straps of my duffel bag since it was as warm as a spring day within the mountain and waited while Rasper the Rabbit tucked away his magical straw and compass and waved at the gate.

An appropriate fanfare for the size and majesty of the gates rang out, heralding our entrance. A lone trumpet blared out a *too-too-do-dooo* welcome. Ky led me through the gates, but I was too busy searching for the trumpet to register all that glittered. There! Finally! Atop one of the pillars sat a smallish fae, perhaps ten times larger than Nessa. The fairy was huffing and puffing, and he only noticed me when he wiped the sweat from his brow. We met eyes but I didn't have the chance to decide whether the fae in his capri britches, suspenders, and sleeveless muscle shirt was friendly before Ky and I emerged on the other side.

My mouth dropped wide open and I didn't care one bit that it revealed exactly how inexperienced I was. "Wow," I whispered, and Ky chuckled, right before someone yelled his name.

"Damn, Ky. What took you so long?" said a guy with brown hair pulled back into a ponytail that rested against the base of his neck. He and Ky came in for one of those bro hugs: clasped hands in an arm-wrestling hold, bumped shoulders, and thumped each other on the back so hard that the smacks sounded hollow.

"We've been waiting for you," the guy said. "We were wondering if you were coming or if you'd chickened out after last term."

Ky scoffed. "Me? Chicken out? I see your sense of humor hasn't improved over the break, Boone. I was really hoping."

Boone chuckled and clamped Ky on the back again. The thump was so loud that I jumped … and noticed someone studying me.

This guy wasn't nearly as rough or relaxed as Boone. His posture was crisp, his steel eyes alert and sharp, and his shoulders were tight in that way that Ky's were when danger was present and he prepared for an attack.

Ky turned toward the guy, but when they greeted there was no rough thumping. They clasped hands and pressed shoulders together, then quickly disbanded.

"Glad to see you," the man with pointy ears and long hair the color of the moon said to Ky, all the while looking at me, his wings tucked in against a strong back. "What took you so long?"

"My little sister. She's a noob. I figured it was my brotherly duty to help her past the Fluffster."

"The Fluffster?" I said with a healthy dose of sarcasm now that I wasn't in fear of immediate dismemberment via rabbit. "Does he have any name that appropriately reflects how creepy he is?"

"You might want to be careful," Silver Hair said in an even, almost curious, tone. "The school hears all, and Rasper is not someone you want to upset."

"Yeah, I already figured that one out, thanks."

The two strangers and I blinked at each other a few times before Ky finally introduced us. "Rina, this is Leander Verion. He's an elfin prince."

Silver Hair was an elfin prince? Holy crap!

He extended his hand toward me, and I wasn't sure if he expected me to shake it or kiss it. Since I wasn't in the business of kissing strangers, I shook it. From the look of surprise that whisked across his face, I suspected he'd wanted me to kiss it. Well, tough cookies, dude.

"And this is Boone," Ky continued. "He's the son and heir to the Northwestern Werewolf Pack alpha."

Dammmn. My brother had set himself up with some *friends* all right.

Boone wrapped a hand around my forearm and grinned. "Welcome, Ky's little sis."

"I'm eighteen," I said right away with a tight smile. "Not so little anymore."

Boone's grin only spread. "And attitude. I like it."

Leander Verion and I scowled, and I wondered why he should care about any of this.

Ky clapped a hand on my shoulder that jerked me. "This is Rina, or as I like to call her, squirt."

"Squirt, huh?" Boone said, and I mentally cataloged all the ways I'd enjoy killing my brother just as soon as I had the opportunity.

I tilted my chin upward toward the three guys, who were all a hand taller than me. "It's Rina, actually. My brother's just being a jerk."

Boone laughed. "Yeah, he's good at it."

I smiled tightly. "If you point me in the right direction, I can be on my way," I told Ky. I really would have preferred that he take me around the school, but this Leander Verion's stare was unnerving, and Boone was as brash as my brother.

Ky's eyes softened, looking like molten copper. "I don't mind showing you around. I can meet up with Leo and Boone later."

"Nah, it's all right," I said just as "Leo" added in an entitled voice:

"She'll be able to find her way."

"Yeah, thanks, *Leander Verion*," I said, hoping he got that my smile was as fake as they came. That whole royalty thing wasn't going to work on me; not a chance. I looked to Ky, who continued to appear concerned, something he rarely was. "Where do I go next, Ky?"

He bit his lip, but finally pointed toward a stately building at the end of a paved path on the left.

"That's the admin building? Acquaine Hall?" I asked.

He nodded.

"Good. Nice to meet you," I said to Leo and Boone, though I wasn't entirely sure it'd been nice, and turned on my heel. I hiked my bag up on my shoulder and started down the appointed path.

I was halfway down it when Ky caught up with me. "I told you I could handle this," I said.

"Yeah, but you were only saying that because of my friends."

"How do you know that?"

"Because I know you. You're my little sister."

"Doesn't mean that's how you have to introduce me to everyone," I said as Ky fell into step next to me. "You're not doing me any favors by making me seem like a puny squirt. And speaking of, you promised!"

"I sure didn't, remember? I specifically didn't promise not to call you 'squirt,' because I can only be so good before it becomes boring, and you know me."

"The quintessential party animal, literally."

He grinned, and his smile was so comforting that I couldn't stay mad at him, though I was pretty sure I should have. Introducing me to an elfin prince and the heir to an alpha position as *squirt*!

Large trees shaded our walk and the day promised to be beautiful and balmy at this secret oasis. "All of this"—I waved my hands at our idyllic surroundings, punctuated by the happy chirping of birds as if we were in a cartoon or something—"this is all magic? Spells control all of it?"

"Every single bit. The Menagerie has a whole team of mages from the Magical Arts Academy that maintain everything here. I'm not gonna lie, it's pretty friggin' awesome."

I took in the perfectly manicured grass and flowerbeds between the many connecting pathways and the constant fresh perfume of nature and had to agree.

"You haven't even seen the best of it yet, Rina," he said. "Trust me. You're about to go on a wild ride."

"Yeah, I think I figured that out on my own."

My brother pulled one of the doors open and

allowed me to enter before him. I narrowed my eyes at him. "What are you up to holding doors for me?"

"Can't I be a good brother to you?"

I only squinted at him more. But then the sights had me looking this way and that, attempting to process as rapidly as my brain could take it all in. "What are they?" I whispered, not wanting to offend the strange creatures that manned the reception area. "They look like trolls, but not like real trolls, like the retro dolls with the pot bellies and fluorescent hair. They even have the hair. They have fro mohawks."

My eyes were wide as I repeated my question. "What are they, Ky? They're so cute!"

"They're pygmy trolls. The dolls were modeled on them."

"No way!"

"Way. Just don't let them catch you calling them 'cute.'"

My throat went dry as the attention of the closest pygmy troll fell on me. I couldn't help but trail my gaze from the bright pink fro-hawk down across a hairless chest the same color as the dolls, and to the desk that shielded the rest of him. "Please tell me they aren't anatomically correct," I whispered.

"No such luck."

I swallowed the thought of pygmy troll junk.

"May I help you?" Pink Fro-Hawk called out, sounding like he shouldn't be in a job where he was required to deal with people.

"Uh, yes." I cleared my throat. "I'm a new

student. I need to check in and get a uniform, I, uh, think."

"You don't need to think. I know my job. Full name?" he asked while other students streamed in behind me and approached some of the equally unfriendly-looking pygmy trolls.

"Ah, um..."

"You do know your name, don't you?"

"Of course. It's Rina Nelle Mont," I said, trying to save face.

Pink Fro-Hawk gave a little jump and disappeared from sight. I rushed to the desk and leaned my forearms over it. The trolls stood on stools.

And I got a full eyeful of little naked troll butt as he stalked to some cabinets and began riffling through file folders. I snapped my gaze away before I could be forever scarred with the full frontal view of the other male trolls who manned the desk—I doubted the skimpy loincloths they wore covered enough—and bumped into my brother.

He was grinning at my discomfort. "Told you you were going to love it here."

It sure beat regular ol' classes at Berry Bramble High, even with my friends there ... assuming I survived the experience.

 ꙮ 5 ꙮ

I STOOD OFF TO THE SIDE OF THE DOOR THAT LED TO the auditorium-style classroom inside Irele Hall and smoothed nonexistent wrinkles from my fresh-out-of-the-package school uniform. The plaid blue pleated skirt and sky-blue button-down shirt were the same as they'd been since the school's founding in 1918. They were stiff and awkward compared to my usual preferred wardrobe of jeans and pull-on shirts, but I wasn't about to complain.

Pink Fro-Hawk had curtly informed me that dorm rooms wouldn't be assigned until the end of the school day to accommodate for students who didn't survive the first day. My duffel bag was secured in a locker in a dressing room off the reception area, where I crossed students who, like me, looked nervous enough to create their own electricity.

As if on cue, a bell trilled throughout the large hall that housed several classrooms and smaller gathering spaces. The bell was softer and more pleasant than the one I was accustomed to from Berry Bramble High, where the bell that announced a change of periods was so loud that it was invariably accompanied by student groans.

But that wasn't the most significant difference. I searched for the origin of the sound, but wasn't surprised when I didn't spot a single sound box anywhere. Not attached to the walls or the ceiling. It was as I'd thought: the bell was magical.

I attempted to hide my creeping grin so as not to broadcast to every passing student that I was a noob. They'd figure that out quickly enough on their own.

I prepared to enter the classroom before the final bell rang, but became distracted by the sea of students bustling by. Ky's classes were in an adjacent hall; I'd already compared his schedule to mine. We had no overlap.

"Rina, what are you doing gaping about like some lost puppy?"

I groaned inwardly before searching for Nessa. When I turned around, my long hair nearly whipped her in the face.

"Whoa!" she said right away. "Watch yourself. You can't just go doing things like that."

"Like what? Turning around? You're the one who was in my face."

Nessa didn't hesitate. "At a school filled to bursting with magical creatures of all sizes, it's your responsibility to watch out for others."

"You're saying I'm supposed to anticipate that a

tiny fairy is flying next to my head every time I turn it?" I asked, deadpan.

"I'm not *tiny*. I'm ... well, never you mind that. What are you doing standing around in the hall? Don't you know your class is about to start? You don't want to be late to class, not ever, and especially not on your first day. Sir Lancelot is almost here. He sent me ahead to get things started."

"Sir Lancelot will be teaching this class?"

"Of course he won't. He has far more important things to do. He manages the entire school, don't you know? And besides, didn't you check your schedule? It should have been mailed to you." Her tiny wings were a blur behind her as she grew more agitated.

"I received my schedule. That's why I'm standing here in front of the door to my first class."

The fairy surveyed me with narrowed eyes as if she were again considering my mental competence.

"I'm about to go in," I said before she could insult me another time.

When she shook her bright blue hair and opened her mouth, I hurried inside before she could say another word.

The classroom was half full, but I suspected I was the last student to enter. Every eye trained on me and I struggled not to physically attempt to shrug off all the attention. My cheeks heated and I concealed my face behind the sheet of hair that slid forward as I looked at the floor, quickly moving across the room to the center aisle. I had to resist the urge to take the steps two at a time as I passed the first rows and headed toward the back.

The entire rear left side of the room was empty, and though my first instinct was to head right for it, that wouldn't do me any favors. I reminded myself that everyone in this room was necessarily new to the school as this was an introduction, and tilted my gaze upward. I landed on two upturned faces that seemed to invite me to join them and I slid into the empty seat next to them, closest to the aisle.

Every head from the front was turned around to continue following me, and I sank in my seat before remembering that I shouldn't reveal my weaknesses. This was a fresh start for me. No point in broadcasting my discomfort. That was a sure recipe for bullies to train a bulls-eye on my back.

"Don't mind them," whispered a girl with jet black hair, one bright white stripe running down the middle of it, while leaning across the girl who separated us. "They're all full of themselves and just trying to make sure you aren't their competition or some shit."

The girl between us nodded her agreement but didn't voice it. She appeared as terrified as I was to be in the midst of so many strangers. Her waist-long hair was shiny brown; her brilliant green eyes reminded me of the thick trees that surrounded the school. But even though she was pretty enough, I could tell she was trying to fade into her surroundings.

"Seriously," White Stripe said. "Ignore them. They'll lose interest in a bit."

"I hope you're right," I muttered, and I was

rewarded with a wicked, wide smile that revealed straight white teeth.

"Oh they will. Trust me on that."

There was something implied in her words, but whatever it was, it was lost on me.

The final bell rang, sounding as if it were inside my head. Several heads besides my own turned toward the corners of the auditorium in an attempt to identify the bell's source. At least I wasn't the only one.

I couldn't help but notice, however, that White Stripe and the girl next to her had trained their eyes on Nessa instead. At the front of the room, flying just above the large desk that crowned the dais of the auditorium, Nessa cleared her throat with a precise *ahem*.

"Attention, everyone," she said, and her tiny voice carried throughout the room, again, as if it were in my head. Magic, it had to be, but how did it work?

Though Dad was a mage, and an accomplished one from what I'd heard from Mom's brothers and sisters, he'd ceased practicing all magic after Mom died, applying his knowledge to the creation of the *Compendium* instead. Magic was nearly as foreign to me as to a human, most of whom were completely in the dark about the existence of both supernatural creatures and the magic that was responsible for them.

Once the whispering silenced to a hush, Nessa continued: "Today you're lucky enough to be welcomed to the school by none other than our illustrious headmaster, Sir Lancelot. He'll be arriving momentarily and I expect that not a one of you will waste a single moment of his time, which is precious, as you all probably already know. Our headmaster's reputation precedes him wherever he goes."

The fairy smiled dreamily before snapping out of it when a hush of chuckles whispered across the front of the room. Nessa snapped her blue head toward the front row and zoomed toward it, where she flew back and forth with the intensity of a wasp about to strike. She pointed at the offending students, all of whom held their heads rigidly straight.

"If a single one of you acts out while Sir Lancelot has the stage, I'm going to sic Fianna on you. And trust me when I tell you, you don't want that."

I looked to White Stripe with a who-the-hell-is-Fianna question on my face, but she was looking at Nessa with apparent fascination. When a grin split her face, I decided she was enjoying the fairy's harassment.

"Fianna will have no problem putting you in your place," Nessa continued. "You get me?"

When no one dared say a word, she repeated, "Am I clear?"

Heads nodded along the first rows and the fairy smiled her triumph. "Good, and just in time. Sir Lancelot is arriving. Please welcome your headmaster!" Her voice rose at the end as if she were a public announcer and we were expected to break out in thunderous applause.

When we received the petite owl in a hush, a frown puckered Nessa's otherwise pleasant face. The owl didn't seem bothered by our reception, however, though the fairy that accompanied him did. If this was

Fianna, then I believed she was capable of meting out punishments as Nessa had suggested. The crimson-haired fairy, though nearly as diminutive as Nessa, emanated a vibe that announced "fierce" as loudly as if she wore a sign that said it.

She whipped in right along with Sir Lancelot, who flew straight for the desk at the head of the room. When the pygmy owl stuck his landing on the desk in near silence, the redheaded fairy and Nessa remained in flight, flanking him on either side like sentinels.

Between the three of them, the owl and fairies couldn't have weighed more than five pounds. But I didn't dare smile. Not even the troublemakers at the front made a peep.

Sir Lancelot faced his audience, tucked his wings behind his back exactly as a person would, and pinned us with large yellow eyes. His brow, covered in brown feathers of varying hues, creased above his eyes, accentuating the humanness of his expression. "Welcome, pupils," he said in a lilting accent that suggested Irish or perhaps Scottish heritage, and just like with the fairy and the school bell, his voice sounded within my head. "Welcome to the Magical Creatures Academy, also referred to as the Menagerie by its students, staff, and alumni, where the brightest and most unique supernatural creatures in the entire world come to study."

He paused and the feathers around his beak tilted upward in what appeared to be a professional smile. "Here, you'll learn how to embrace the extent of your powers. You'll come to understand the full range of your magic under the tutelage of some of the finest teachers in the supernatural community, many of whom are themselves graduates of the Menagerie. Those that aren't are likely graduates of our sister institution, the Magical Arts Academy."

The two fairies nodded alongside him.

"The course load at the Menagerie is intense. This isn't the place for the lazy or the incompetent. You'll be expected to give your all while you're here. You'll be pushed and challenged to your full capacity. Nothing about the course you're about to embark upon is easy; don't be fooled. If you expected easy, then there's the exit." The owl pointed at the open door with a wingtip. "If you expected to come here and snooze, you'll be disappointed."

Those wide yellow eyes traveled across the room. "Look to the student to your right."

I turned to face the quiet girl with the willowy brown hair next to me.

"Now look to your left." I was relieved to get to stare across the aisle to empty seats.

"Statistically, one of those two students won't make it through to summer. Exactly half of those of you in this room won't advance to second term. One of two of you won't be able to handle the workload not just *expected* of you, but *demanded* of you." The owl allowed his final words to ring out.

"All of you in this room possess the basic qualities to be exemplary students of the Menagerie. If not, the school's magic wouldn't have selected you. But just because you meet the elementary requirements in no way means you have what it takes to succeed here. The school is the finest there is for a supernatural creature. In fact, it's argued that it's the only acceptable institution for the supernatural."

Again, he peered across the sea of pupils staring back at him. "Only the strongest among you will persevere. Only the best and brightest of you will advance to the next term. And only the most brilliant of you all will make it to the ninth and final term to graduate from the school. If you are one of those fortunate enough to make it to the end, you'll have the supernatural community's respect, and opportunities will be yours for the claiming. You'll be equipped to positively contribute to the supervisory efforts of the Enforcers during your required apprenticeship with them. You'll be fully empowered and ready to enter the world at large as a prime contributor to it."

The owl swept a wing in our general direction. "You all begin as equals. There isn't a single one of you here who is better—or worse—than the other. The school has chosen you because you possess the necessary magic within you to succeed in this competitive environment. Whether you do or not is entirely up to how much you want the triumph, to how much you're willing to place all of yourself on the line to give what is required to graduate from the most highly distinguished school for creatures. You alone will determine what happens during your time here. You have nine semesters ahead of you to complete the curriculum for graduation."

Even the fairies pinned their attention on us. My

skin tingled at all the intensity traveling across the expanse of the auditorium.

"Make the most of your time here and you'll never regret it. Waste it, and the school will kick you out just as eagerly as it invited you to be a part of it. Magic monitors every part of the school's functioning. There will be no grades, no percentages, no nonsense. The spell that guides the school sees all and knows all. You have only to prove yourself to the Menagerie and to yourself. Be sure not to let either down."

I swallowed loudly. No wonder Ky hadn't told me much about the school. If he had, I might not have gathered the courage to attend. As I was already here, there was nothing to do but give it everything I had, just as Sir Lancelot tasked.

This was my one chance at becoming the one thing I'd longed to be since my first memories. I was probably the only one who hadn't yet manifested her powers. I was already a step behind. I just had to hope that wasn't enough to knock me out of the running.

I nodded my head in determination. I'd never taken on a challenge this significant. I hoped I was ready … despite appearances.

❧ 6 ❧

AFTER SIR LANCELOT'S WELCOME SPEECH, WHICH LEFT the students shuffling and shifting uncomfortably in their seats, the owl's demeanor transformed. Absent was the severe owl, replaced with one who appeared several centuries younger than his rumored thousand-plus years.

"To begin, you'll be divided into groups," he said, and I had flashbacks to high school PE and dreading being the last one to be picked for a team. "As your studies advance, your assigned group will change and will be determined according to various factors, including skill set and natural tendencies. Until those become clear to your teachers, however, you'll be divided into three basic categories: vampires, shapeshifters, and other, the latter group including any creatures who do not shift form but naturally maintain the form at all times."

I scanned the crowd but didn't see any critters. All human-looking students.

"If you're neither a vampire nor a shapeshifter, please join the 'other' group, and your teacher will sort you out. Of course there are many of you who don't fit into neat categories, but don't fret, the 'other' category will suit you just fine. It's only because your numbers are smaller that we group you into one overarching category."

A flush of heat swept across my body, but before I had the chance to figure out what group I belonged in, three men entered the room, demanding all my attention.

"Perfect timing," the owl said, his voice humming with contentment. I had the feeling the headmaster relished the smooth functioning of his school. "Students, these are your group leaders. They'll be the ones to assess you and guide you during much of your first term here."

Sir Lancelot gestured at the men with a wing. "Come, gentlemen. Take your places in front of the desk, where the pupils can see you."

The oddest pairing of men I'd ever seen crossed the auditorium and took their places in front of the dais, raised above floor level by a foot.

Sir Lancelot nodded his approval, then pointed to the first man. "This is Professor Lorenzo Damante. He is the leader of the vampire group."

After seeing Professor Damante, I was certain I'd never seen another vamp before, or at least I'd never observed one who was this refined. The man, who appeared to be in his mid-forties but likely wasn't, wore his clothing like a runway model, if runway models looked as if they could snap you in half without breaking a sweat. His jet black hair accentuated his pale skin, enhancing his high cheekbones and bright lips.

But Professor Damante's eyes were what captivated me. Vampires were supposed to be able to lure their victims to their peril with just one look. Professor Damante's coal black eyes convinced me it was true.

"Professor Damante is special," White Stripe whispered when she noticed me glancing toward the large windows, which admitted enough light to reduce a whole host of vampires to dust. "He isn't affected by light the way other vamps are. He—"

But she stopped when Sir Lancelot continued. Even White Stripe was unwilling to miss a word the owl said.

"This is Professor Conan McGinty. He'll lead the shapeshifter group."

Professor McGinty was a very large, very strong-looking man. The shifter was as imposing as the vamp, but in an entirely different way. While the vamp appeared to be constantly moving pieces around on a proverbial chessboard, the shifter looked like he grabbed life by the horns and rode it hard. As solid as a tree trunk, with a head of unruly auburn hair and a full beard to match, whatever McGinty shifted into must be formidable.

"And last but certainly not least," the owl continued, "is Professor Burl Quickfoot. He'll be guiding the 'other' group."

Obviously. Professor Quickfoot was definitely

something else. I edged forward in my seat to see him better. He was either a very small man, or maybe a dwarf?

"Professor Quickfoot is not only one of the finest gnomes among his people, but also a master at a variety of different supernatural creatures, especially the woodland ones. He's the best bet you have if you don't fit neatly into the other categories, much as I don't."

The owl offered a smile apparently meant to soothe those of us who were different. It helped, but only a little. I shifted in my seat.

"Now that you're in capable hands, I'll take my leave. There's a pesky little matter I must attend to at once." After one final scan of the pupils assembled before him, the pygmy owl, who was at most six inches tall, gave a curt, satisfied nod, and flew out the door in one swoop. The two fairies trailed behind him, slower than the owl, but no less determined.

All eyes then fell on the three mismatched professors at the front of the auditorium.

Ky had told me not knowing who or what I was wouldn't be an issue. He'd said it was no big deal, that lots of students arrived at the Menagerie with little knowledge of what they were.

He'd lied.

"ALL RIGHT, EVERYONE," McGINTY BOOMED. "YOU heard the commander. Chip-chop, let's get to it."

Along with most of the other students, I scrambled to my feet. The shifter's voice was loud and firm and my instinct was to obey whatever it said. The willowy girl who sat next to me popped to her feet as well, but White Stripe didn't, and I offered her a curious look, one she met with a mischievous wink.

The girl was trouble, I could already tell. She uncurled her legs from where they were tucked beneath her body on the cushy fold-up seat and rose languorously. Willowy Girl and I were already a third of the way down the stairs of the center aisle when she caught up to us.

"Shifters, join me," McGinty called. "Vamps join Professor Damante. If you don't fit into either category, find Professor Quickfoot."

Damante and Quickfoot separated from McGinty. The vamp moved under the tall windows, leaned against the wall, and folded his arms across his chest as if he were posing for the cover of GQ. His charcoal suit, pressed bright blue shirt with the top two buttons undone, and shiny black shoes were immaculate.

White Stripe chuckled behind me, and I turned to look over my shoulder with a question on my face.

"He's so arrogant," she said so softly that I had to strain to hear her. "He's flaunting that he isn't affected by sunlight. He also has superb hearing."

I looked from White Stripe to Damante. His black eyes flicked up to meet mine at that exact moment. But they didn't move to White Stripe, who'd been the one to criticize him. He held my gaze until I gulped, then finally looked away.

I breathed out, noticed I'd stopped moving, and advanced only to find that my legs were a bit wobbly.

"That was a close one," Willowy Girl whispered directly in my ear.

I desperately wanted to ask the soft-spoken girl what she meant, but she continued descending the stairs without me.

Professor Quickfoot chose the area in front of the open door, and a few students made their way to him.

In fact, every student moved with purpose. All but Willowy Girl and me.

White Stripe passed us to move toward McGinty. But Willowy Girl hesitated, looking between McGinty and Quickfoot several times before nodding her head and moving up the center toward McGinty.

I hesitated until I once again sensed the attention of everyone on me like an itchy rash that swept across my skin. Now that I'd experienced Damante's gaze, I identified him as one of those who studied me. I refused to meet his eyes or those of anyone else.

I bit my lip and worked not to fidget—or better yet, to flee the room.

McGinty called out, "If you don't know where ya fit, then maybe Professor Quickfoot's group is the best." He pretended he wasn't singling me out, though it was clear that he had to be.

The room grew completely silent, save the subtle sounds of students rustling in their uniforms. Time ticked by so noticeably that I swore I could actually hear it in my head, much like the bells.

"Any time now," a boy's voice said from where

Professor Damante held court, and a few snickers followed. I ignored them, though sweat erupted along my underarms. All I needed now were sweat stains.

I let out a huff of a breath, then moved toward the gnome and his tall, red, pointed hat.

Halfway to him, I swerved and approached McGinty.

The shifter's eyes trailed every one of my movements until I stood directly in front of him. When I took my place next to White Stripe and Willowy Girl, he raised dark red eyebrows at me.

I gave one curt nod and straightened my shoulders. I might be quivering inside, but I didn't need to make it so easy for everyone to deduce it.

Odds were high that I was a shifter. I wasn't a mage like Dad or the Magical Arts Academy would have been the one to come calling instead of the Menagerie. Ky was a shifter, as Mom had been. Though it wasn't a guarantee that my magic was similar to theirs—when it came to magic, there were no guarantees—it was probable since I was here.

"This is all of us, then," McGinty said, his eyes still on me. "Shifters, all of you?"

I didn't visibly react right away, and Willowy Girl raised her hand.

"Yes?" McGinty said, amused.

"Well, Professor, I'm not entirely sure where I belong."

"Do you shift, lass?"

"I do."

"Then you belong here."

"It doesn't matter what I shift into?"

"No. Any animal will do."

Willowy Girl fidgeted many different ways at once. She crossed her arms over her stomach, stood one foot atop the other, and blew at the chunk of hair that fell in her face.

"What do you shift into if not an animal?" McGinty asked, face alight with curiosity.

"I, uh, well, I turn into a ... a tree."

"A tree?" the teacher barked far too suddenly and far too loudly, though I didn't think he'd meant to embarrass the girl.

Her cheeks turned a rosy pink, and I was grateful for an instant that everyone's attention was on her instead of me, before I felt like crap for thinking it.

Before I could debate the wisdom of outing myself to the class, I said, "I don't know what I turn into." As the mass attention shifted to me, I lowered my voice. "I, um, well, I'm pretty sure I'm a shifter."

"What makes you so sure?" McGinty asked.

"My mother was a shifter, and so's my brother."

McGinty shook his head, the mass of hair atop it moving wildly. "You could take after your father."

"He's a mage."

"A mage, you say?"

I nodded and tilted my head downward a little until my hair slid to hide my reddening cheeks.

"Hmm, let me get this straight, lassie. Are you telling me that you've never shifted?"

My throat went dry. "That's right," I squeaked.

"So what's your magic like, then? We might be able to tell from that alone."

"Um…" I looked around the room. Not a single student or teacher appeared apologetic to be staring at me. "I, um … I don't know."

My confession was followed by a deep and encompassing silence. I was sure the entire class could hear my thumping heartbeat.

"Then what's she doing here?" the same student voice as before called out from the vamp area.

"Yeah," echoed a girl's voice from the same location. "If she doesn't have magic, she doesn't belong."

"That's enough," said Professor Quickfoot, and I shot him a grateful look he was sure to see since I was bright as his hat by now. "Conan, you take her for now. She can always join me later if your group isn't a good fit." The gnome's voice was deep and surprisingly soothing, and I didn't think it was just because he was bringing my mortification to a swift end.

"That'll work," McGinty said to the gnome, who then turned to lead his students from the auditorium. I managed to spot the red of his hat from between their moving legs a few times, but beyond that, the students dwarfed their teacher. But they didn't dwarf his power. Those few words he'd spoken continued to affect me, and I half wished I'd chosen his group instead of the shifter's.

But then White Stripe bumped shoulders with me, and Willowy Girl offered me a humiliated smile that I could relate to, and I decided I'd made the right choice—for now, anyway.

Professor Damante swept in front of the group of shifters with a lasting scrutiny of me that didn't slow his sure, strong strides. The students who trailed him were Mini-Me's of the vamp, oozing the potential for deadly sophistication, even amid their taunts.

One of the vamps, a boy with eyes as calculating as Damante's but far more wicked, bumped into me. I shot forward, stumbling, before catching myself.

"Oops, I'm sorry," the kid said. "My bad." His eyes appeared to swirl and I wanted to turn away from him.

I refused and glared.

He laughed, tossed his head to adjust the wave of hair atop it, and caught up with the three boys who waited on him. Before exiting the room, he and another cast a final look at me.

"They're gonna get it," White Stripe whispered, though I was certain McGinty must have heard her.

"Wait," I said, "why were the kids able to stand under the windows with light streaming in?"

"Oh, girl, you really don't know much about the supernatural community, do you? Vamps aren't activated in the same way shifters are. They have to undergo a whole blood ritual to become full-blooded vamps. Until then, they're more human than after. After ... well, let's just say that after they're even less likeable."

Less likeable? That shouldn't be possible.

"All right, shifters," McGinty said in his boomy voice that carried. "Let's roll. It's time to teach you about your powers so no one can push you around."

He didn't lock eyes with any of us, but he was talking to Willowy Girl and me, for sure.

When he stalked toward the door with a grace that shouldn't have been possible for a man his size, I didn't hesitate to follow. It was time to figure out my strengths—any of them. Anything at all to smooth over my time at the Menagerie.

Because apparently there were some things you didn't leave behind when you abandoned the human world. Mean people were everywhere.

At least I'd never have to see a particular clique of snotty girls from Berry Bramble High ever again, and that relief went a long way to make up for the occasional pangs of nostalgia when I thought of my friends back home. Too bad the Menagerie had its own clique of mean people, and this one had a thirst for blood.

I intended to be one of the half that made it through the academy, which meant I had to learn to stand up for myself. I wouldn't let nasty people take me down.

7

PROFESSOR DAMANTE LED THE VAMPS FARTHER INSIDE Irele Hall. McGinty turned in the opposite direction, leading our group of shifters through the large double doors to the outside.

Willowy Girl cast a grateful look to the retreating back of the vamps. I leaned toward her. "I feel you," I said, and she smiled at me and nodded.

"Don't worry, girls," White Stripe said as the three of us brought up the rear of our group. "We've got this."

"I'd like to think so," I said, but dragged my words out.

"Then think so." She scrunched her face up into a smile, waggled her nose, making her nose ring wiggle, and winked through thick black eyeliner and mascara. "Trust yourselves."

"Is it so obvious that we don't? That I don't, I mean. Sorry," I offered to Willowy Girl.

"Nah, it's all right. It's true. It isn't easy being a tree when everyone else is a wolf or a bear or something else cool."

"Tell me about it," I muttered.

White Stripe was looking at us oddly when McGinty stopped walking and turned around. "Gather round, everyone. We're far enough away from Burl that we won't bother him."

He was right. Professor Quickfoot had veered in the opposite direction and stood at the base of a large, old tree, his crimson hat just barely peeking out above the heads of the students seated on the ground in front of him. Even with his hat on, he was only waist height.

Willowy Girl, White Stripe, and I joined the rest of the shifters—an odd dozen or so, including us— and sat criss-cross-applesauce on the ground, a bit damp from the nighttime dew. At least the enchantments that created an oasis in the middle of an arid desert included weather modification. Though it was January and bitter cold everywhere else in Sedona, here it was pleasant, especially since McGinty had chosen a spot the tall trees that dotted the school grounds didn't shade. The mid-morning sun warmed me, helping to settle my nerves, and I lifted my face toward it.

Until I sensed eyes on me—McGinty. As if he were trying to figure me out. *Well, go ahead, bud. Have at it.*

I fussed with tucking my skirt in around my legs so

I wasn't flashing my new teacher and waited for him to start. But he continued to study me.

Ky was so going to get it. He hadn't told me I'd be an oddball like this. Even the teachers were overcome by my differences.

When McGinty began to speak, his eyes remained on me. "All right, so here we are. You've heard Sir Lancelot's warnings. I won't bother repeating 'em. I wish I could say he's exaggerating, but he isn't."

When tension bloomed among our troop, he added, "That's why it's your lucky day that you're a shifter and you're in my group. I won't stop until every single one of you succeeds. The only way to fail in this group is by giving up. If you're trying the best you can, then you're doing all you need to be doing in my group. I'll tell you there's a problem if I think there's one, so don't create problems that don't exist. You'll fail a hundred times. As long as you get up a hundred and one, you're doing just fine."

He clapped his large hands together, making Willowy Girl and me jump. White Stripe chuckled.

"My job is to guide you so that you understand your shifter form, begin to work with the power of it, and learn all you can about yourself before the term is over. Obviously you won't learn everything there is to learn about your alternate shape from now until May. There's a reason you have to complete nine terms to graduate. There's much more to being a shifter than learning about your other form. You'll also need to understand how you fit into the magical world at large, what your duties are to protect our kind and the vulnerable humans—especially now that the supernatural world is in such turmoil and the Enforcers are overworked trying to keep rogue shifters and vamps under control. There's more to learn about the world of magic than you can possibly imagine at this point in your studies. Nine semesters might sound like a lot to you now, but I promise you, they aren't. Which is one of the reasons why I don't believe in wasting time, and believe you me, neither does Sir Lancelot.

"Before we do anything, I need to know your names and your shifter shapes. I realize you've all turned eighteen sometime in the last four months, and that's not a lot of time, so don't worry if your shift isn't smooth. That's not what we're after—yet."

"He isn't going to make us shift in front of the class, is he?" I asked White Stripe in a hushed, terrified whisper.

I expected her to grin in response, enjoying my discomfort, but she scowled and picked at the clasps on her black Doc Martens' Mary Jane's. "He's definitely going to make us shift," she grumped.

As if he'd heard her, something that was entirely possible depending on what kind of hearing the supernatural possessed, McGinty pointed to her and said, "Let's start with you."

"Me?" White Stripe said.

"Yeah, you." The glint to the professor's eyes seemed like some sort of challenge.

White Stripe groaned loudly, stood, and dragged her feet as she made her way to the front, moving among the seated students instead of going around, so as to cause maximum disruption. She faced us with a scowl. "My name's Jasmine, but for the love of gooey homemade chocolate chip cookies straight from the oven, don't call me that. Not unless you want to be on my shit list." She flicked eyes to McGinty. "Am I allowed to say that here?"

"I think you'll soon find that a little cussing is the least of our problems at the Menagerie."

Well, that was reassuring.

But Jasmine-who-wasn't-Jasmine nodded her appreciation. "Call me Jas"—she pronounced it like *Jazz*. "My parents are assholes. You'll soon see why." She tucked chin-length hair behind her ear. "What else do you need me to say?"

"Whatever you want. But especially what you transform into and how long you've been able to shift."

"Okay. I turned eighteen in the middle of September, which means I've had to wait to attend until the next term rolled around, which was forever." She rolled her eyes, a blue lighter than any I'd ever seen, unless it was the dark eye makeup making it seem that way. "I shifted immediately, of course. And lo and behold, I'm a ... I'm a skunk."

She looked out at the grouping of students with a ferocious look on her face, daring anyone to make fun of her. Since she looked a bit deranged, and like she could kick the crap out of anyone who dared to taunt her, no one did—proof that size wasn't everything. Jas couldn't be more than five-foot-two and slim, with a mostly flat chest, but she looked like the kind of girl you'd want on your side in an alley fight—mean and wily when she wanted to be.

Even McGinty waited until he'd properly stashed away his surprise to speak. "A skunk, huh?"

Jas nodded with the sort of calm that brewed storms and clenched and unclenched her fists at her sides.

"Skunk shifters aren't common."

"No, they aren't. Lucky me."

"I don't see why it wouldn't be lucky," McGinty said. "No animal form is lesser than. Size and type doesn't determine much unless the shifter knows how to use their magic. Besides, magic is never by accident. If you're a skunk, then there's a very good reason for it. Is either of your parents a skunk? Or anyone else in your family?"

"No. I'm the only skunk. My mom shifts into a possum, and my dad's a raccoon."

"A family of medium-sized mammals, then. Very well, though all that matters is what you are. Show us what you've got, Jas."

Jas nodded sharply, then closed her eyes. I took advantage of the opportunity to study the feisty shifter, and discovered that she was actually pleasant looking when her face relaxed, once you looked past the heavy eye makeup. A tiny diamond-looking gem dangled and sparkled from the hoop of her gold nose ring.

The edges of her body began to blur, the first indication that a shift was impending. I recognized the signs from Ky, though with him the shift was so fast nowadays that I only noticed the blurring when I was looking for it.

Next came the vibrating, so that it appeared her body was shaking, followed by her body flickering in and out of focus. And then, *poof!* She was a large skunk. The entire process took no more than a minute.

The school uniform, complete with her own flair of fishnet stockings, disappeared along with the girl, and in her place was a skunk with rich black fur and a thick white stripe down the middle of her back. Her bushy tail was all white and looked silky soft.

Skunky Jas, despite appearing cute and feminine even though three times the size of a normal skunk, bared sharp teeth and claws, as if daring anyone to laugh at the skunk named after a fragrant flower.

"Calm it down, Jas," McGinty said. "No one's gonna hurt you."

But Jas merely restrained herself to a few snarls before prancing back and forth in front of us a couple of times. Her bushy white tail waved as she walked, reminding me of a curvaceous woman swaying her hips in seduction. I'd never tell Jas that, though; I liked myself in one piece.

"All right. That's great. Go ahead and shift back."

I trained my eyes on the giant skunk, but Jas' shift back to human was even faster than it was the other way around. She was a skunk, I blinked a few times, and then she was back to herself, the edges of her body solid and complete. Her uniform was as fresh as it'd been before she shifted.

She flicked the white stripe in her hair to the side and cut a straight path between the students seated on the ground, forcing them to lean out of her way. Then she plopped between Willowy Girl and me at the back.

"That was some excellent shifting," McGinty said, ignoring her aggression and nodding in approval. "You've obviously been practicing. It takes most shifters several terms to have that much control. You're ahead of the game, lass. Good job."

Jas nodded and cleared her throat nervously when her pale cheeks flushed. When she caught me looking at her, she barked, "What?"

"Nothing. That was awesome," I said. "I wish I could do that."

"Become a smelly skunk?"

I shrugged. "I thought you were pretty awesome. You weren't smelly, you were pretty."

"Pretty?" she snarled.

"Right," I scrambled. "Not pretty. Totally vicious looking. Those claws! And those teeth. I was terrified."

She glared at me until the façade cracked. "Terrified. Yeah, right," she said on a chortle.

I shrugged. "You looked like you could tear some shit up."

"Oh, I can. Trust me on that."

"Good job, Jas," Willowy Girl said from her other side.

"Yeah, whatever."

I smiled. Jas was going to be a trip, no doubt about it.

"Next," McGinty called, and we went through a

standard werewolf, a bear on the smallish side, a coyote, and several smaller animals, including a cotton-tailed bunny, which proved that Jas' animal wasn't the meekest of the bunch. Several of my class-mates struggled with their shifts, but McGinty only encouraged them along until they fully transformed. All of them took longer to achieve a complete shift than Jas had, and many of them seemed shaken from the process.

"You," McGinty said, pointing to an average-looking boy with brown hair, brown eyes, medium height and build. Nothing about his features made him either nice or bad looking, but his smile was kind and true enough to make me instantly like him.

"My name's Dave Bailey and I shift into a bobcat. My birthday's in December, so I've only been shifting for a couple of weeks." The plain boy appeared perfectly comfortable in his own skin; that made me like him even more. "No one in my family is a bobcat, so no one's sure what happened there. I guess I just got lucky." He smiled.

"Lucky indeed, lad," McGinty said. "Bobcats are pretty cool creatures. I've met one or two over the years. Beautiful animals. Are you sized like an ordi-nary one?"

"Precisely. There's nothing uncommon about my cat. I'm pretty sure most people wouldn't notice any differences between me and others."

"That's a handy advantage in a world where stealth and the ability to blend in are as important as power."

Dave nodded, his neatly-trimmed brown hair sliding around pleasantly. "Ready for me to shift?"

"Be my guest."

"All right. Just to warn y'all, I'm still not all that good at it, so beware."

Beware of what? It's not as if a shift gone wrong could hurt any of us, could it?

Dave repeated the identical steps the rest of the shifters had gone through, but with nowhere near the finesse Jas had displayed. His edges didn't blur exactly; it was more like they cracked, and the missing pieces of his body kept appearing and then vanishing again. It took at least five minutes for him to progress to the stage where his body began to shake, but when he reached it, I almost wished he hadn't.

His body trembled so violently that his teeth chattered in his head, and I worried he might get a concussion from all the rattling around his brain must be doing in his skull. When his eyes widened in what appeared to be terror, McGinty edged toward him as if to intervene. But Dave wasn't a quitter, and he continued on even after he bit his tongue from all the thrashing.

When his body finally began to flash—there one second, gone for a millisecond, then back again—I was dreading my own shift. Since my birthday I'd wanted nothing but to shift. After seeing Dave, and to some degree the rest of the students too, I wasn't sure shifting was as amazing as I'd envisioned.

I hugged my knees to my chest before remembering I was in a skirt instead of jeans and couldn't do that. Willowy Girl offered me a look that said, *It won't be all that bad, really.* But how on earth could she know that? We didn't even know what I'd shift into, assuming I could even shift. Just because the Menagerie's magic had never made a mistake before didn't mean I couldn't be the first.

With my luck, I definitely could be the first mistake in a century.

Then Dave finally shifted into his bobcat with a warbled pop that wasn't quite right. I leaned forward from my seat on the ground to get a better look.

"Oh no," McGinty said, scrambling for a better response. "Not to worry, students. This is a common problem for new shifters."

Holy hell, then I really didn't want to shift.

"It will be fine, and this will all be sorted out once Dave gets more experience."

But for now Dave had the head of a bobcat ... on the body of a teenage boy—mostly. His hands and feet were paws as wide as his hands, and a tail popped out from the waistband of his solid-blue uniform pants.

"At least his head is still the right size," Willowy Girl said, and I had to agree. It could've been worse.

"I haven't gotten it quite right," Dave said, his voice cattier than usual. He licked his whiskers and blinked cat eyes with slanted pupils.

"That's all right, lad. No problem. As I said, shifting takes patience and practice to get it just right." But McGinty's usual cool was absent, and he was speaking faster than he had at the start. "You're doing a great job." McGinty nodded a little too enthusiastically. "But let's have you shift back for now until we can get you sorted out."

Dave squeezed his eyes shut for several minutes, but nothing happened. When he peeked one eye open, I knew it was bad news. "I think I'm stuck," he said.

McGinty twisted his mouth in his beard as if after however many years of teaching this was a first. But then he got himself together and said, "Right. Well, then, off to Melinda we go. The badger can fix just about anything. She's a genius."

I was pretty sure every student hinged on the "just about anything" part of his comment.

"The bell's about to ring anyway. We'll convene again tomorrow and get to it first thing. Class dismissed."

None of the students budged until McGinty led a half boy, half bobcat off in the direction of the healing wing.

When the other students began to rise to head off to their next classes, Willowy Girl and I shared a wide-eyed look.

"That means we'll be going tomorrow," she said.

I gulped. "It looks like it."

Ky had definitely omitted this particular danger of shifting. What if I got stuck in between a girl and whatever I was too? That was just the kind of thing I'd do.

"No point worrying about something that might not even happen, girls," Jas said. "I have Beginning Creature History 101 next period. How about you?"

"Same," we said.

"Excellent. Then let's go before grass grows under our asses."

Jas popped to standing, and Willowy Girl soon followed. I had no choice but to continue on with my day and pretend I wasn't already dreading tomorrow.

8

THE MOMENT WREN—WILLOWY GIRL—JAS, AND I entered the dining hall, I immediately realized the experience of eating was going to be just as intimidating as the rest of my first day of school. The large hall, though half empty, echoed chaos. I flinched instinctively, resisting the desire to turn tail and run the other way.

There were too many people in here. Or actually, there were too many creatures, and every single one of them held a potentially dangerous secret, guaranteed.

Wren sidled closer to me as she and I hesitated just inside the double doors. Jas continued on without us but whirled on us when she noticed we weren't right behind her.

She gave us a look that I suspected suggested we were cowards, then huffed and stomped back toward us. "Are you waiting for an invitation or something? Come on. I'm hungry."

My stomach growled in agreement and my cheeks flushed.

Jas, of course, laughed. "You either have a beast inside you or you're just as hungry as I am. After Beginning Creature History, I need some fuel to pep me up, that's for sure." She groaned and rolled her eyes. "I mean, could there be a more boring teacher? I really don't think so."

She turned again and set off toward the far walls, two of which were lined with food offerings. This time, she didn't check whether we followed, and Wren and I fell into line before she could get too far ahead of us. I wasn't sure I'd have the guts to take on the dining hall without her.

We marched between long wooden tables. Jas carried her head high, not bothering to glance at anyone, even though several of the seated students looked up. I worked to imitate her confidence and failed. I focused on not tripping on my own feet and making a fool of myself before the first day was over.

Mesmerized by the many distinct aromas wafting from the food and the many options offered in pan after pan, I slammed to a stop when I noticed who manned the buffets.

Wren bumped into me when I stuttered in mid-step. "What is it?" she asked, looking around with wide, soft eyes.

Jas was leaving us behind and I hurried to catch up, Wren on my heels. "Nothing, it's just the, um, trolls. I wasn't expecting them." Because, come on, who'd expect to see pygmy trolls manning the food station?

"I get it," Wren said. "They make me nervous too."

They more than made me nervous. They totally unnerved me, and my interaction with Pink Fro-hawk hadn't helped.

Jas moved off to the side to let some other students who came up behind us pass. "What are you guys going to have? I can't decide between the pizza and the Chinese food. They both look awesome. Or maybe I should have a sub..."

She seemed oblivious to our discomfort. At this point, I didn't much care what I ate as long as what was serving the food didn't eat me.

"I'm going to have the stir-fry," Wren said, casting a nervous look at me and sidling up to the counter closest to us.

I was with her. Get in, get out, stay alive. "I'll have that too," I said, and joined her.

Jas shrugged. "It was one of the things I was considering anyway," and she moved next to us.

My entire body relaxed by a fraction when she got into line with us. Was I hiding behind her bravado? Yes, yes I was, and I wasn't the least bit ashamed of it. I had the feeling much of my time at the Menagerie would be focused on simple survival.

A pygmy troll approached the counter from the other side, narrowed his eyes at the three of us, and said, "What do you want?"

Jas, of course, was the only one not to jump at

the gravel that was his voice. "I'd like the spicy Schezuan vegetables with hot and sour sauce on the side."

I had no idea if I'd like that, but I said, "I'd like the same please," and Wren nodded beside me, a bit too enthusiastically. "Me too," she said, and we took a joint step back while we waited.

Jas leaned on the counter with her hip and crossed her arms across her chest. "You two are something, you know that?"

I nodded even though I was sure she didn't mean we were a special kind of something in a good way. My gaze skittered between her and the grumpy troll, who squeezed oil from a squirt bottle into an oversized wok, dumped a vegetable medley into it, and squeezed some sauce from another bottle on top of the mixture —all without moving his hands, the ones that numbered four fingers instead of five.

He popped up onto a stool in front of the large stove, bent over, and blew on the burner. It burst into flame, and I got an eyeful of round pygmy troll butt that wasn't concealed by the apron that only covered the front.

I wanted to look away, I *really* did, but the sight of the small ornery troll with blue fluorescent hair tamped beneath a hair net was close to being one of the most interesting things I'd seen all day.

"You'd better not let him catch you staring," Jas said, amused, but softly enough that it might not catch the troll's attention.

I jerked my gaze away from the troll to meet Jas'

dancing eyes. "This is going to take some getting used to," I said. Wren nodded eagerly beside me.

Jas tilted her head this way and that, considering. "What's up with you two? It's like you've never seen supernaturals before or something." When neither of us said a thing, her eyes widened again, at least three coats of mascara making her eyes shockingly bright. "You have seen supernaturals before, right?"

"More or less," I said as Wren said, "Barely."

Jas huffed, sending the white stripe of hair flying from where it'd rested against her forehead. "We have lots to talk about, then, it'd seem." To the troll, she said, "Hey, hurry it up, will ya? We haven't got all day."

The blue-haired troll, who looked like he was missing an appendage with his hair flattened against his head, turned beady eyes on Jas. "You think food cooks faster just 'cause you tell it to?"

"It might if you use your troll magic on it."

"Troll magic is special," he grumbled. "Not for just any ol' thing."

"Fine. I get it." She feigned nonchalance. "You have to be really powerful to use troll magic whenever you want. You don't have enough troll magic to spare. No problem. We'll just wait as long as it takes."

"I'm plenty powerful," he grumbled, stirring the food in jerky, stabbing movements—sans utensils.

Jas shrugged and gave him a bland smile.

"I am. I have lots of magic."

"I'm sure you do." Her smile widened into a blasé thing, and the troll's piercing eyes flared. I inched closer to Wren and away from the crazy skunk shifter with an apparent death wish.

"I do. I'll prove it."

"No need. I believe you," she said in the voice that one used when one didn't believe someone.

The troll's features, which already reminded me of a *bah humbug* little old man, scrunched until his face was mostly crinkled skin and a large, bulbous nose. It would have been comical if not for the fact that this wasn't an it's-so-ugly-it's-cute Troll Doll that you could put on a shelf.

He smacked a hand to one of his hips, jutted it to the side, and gave a watch-this-sucker head tilt, smirk firmly in place. Without bothering to look at the searing wok, he extended his other hand toward the pan and flashed magic that matched the color of his hair—the azure of cotton candy.

The fire of the burner flared to alarming heights, our food spit and sizzled, and then—still without breaking Jas' gaze—he waved his hand before clenching it into a fist like a composer who was bringing his musicians to the end of a piece.

"And that's how troll magic is done," he said, opening his fist and hovering the food from the wok and guiding it over three plates, where he let it plop as if it were slop. The plates floated toward us and smacked against our side of the counter, spilling a few pieces of broccoli and a couple of carrots in the process.

I snatched up my plate. "Thanks so very much," I

said, my words tumbling out far too fast. "That was awesome. It looks delicious. I can't wait to eat."

"Yeah, thanks," Wren echoed, clutching her plate against her stomach.

We swiveled on our heels and marched off, grabbing utensils and a drink before heading toward the table farthest from the blue-haired troll. I plopped onto the empty bench seat and my entire body melted. "Holy crap," I said, and Wren, who appeared as shell-shocked as I felt, nodded, eyes still wide as if they were stuck in that position. "The girl has a death wish," she said. "I don't know much, but even I know not to bother the trolls."

Jas arrived and slid her plate onto the table next to us. "Could you guys have picked a more isolated table?" she said like nothing had happened. "If you're going to make friends here, this isn't the way."

"I'm pretty sure your way isn't the way either," I said. "What were you thinking with that troll?"

She shrugged and took a bite, rolling her eyes. "Man, was I hungry. This is actually good."

"We're lucky the troll didn't spit in our food or something after how you treated him."

Wren nodded her agreement; she did a lot of that. "He probably would've if we hadn't been watching him."

Jas took another bite and waved a hand. "He was fine. I was just messing with him, and he knew it."

"Yeah, I'm pretty sure he got that you were messing with him," I said, ignoring my food.

She smiled. "He did get pretty riled up, didn't he?"

"You actually think that's funny?"

"Yeah, I do. They like the banter. Trust me, they're always grumps. They like the interaction, keeps them on their toes, and it keeps it from getting boring. That troll was glad I got him all fired up. It probably made his day."

"Maybe if you mean it in a Dirty Harry 'Make my day' kind of way," I said.

Apparently bored by Wren's and my concern with surviving our dining hall experience while students at the Menagerie, Jas took in our surroundings. "Everyone else must be checking on dorm assignments, huh? I figured everyone would've rushed here after class. Shifting requires extra fuel. After class with McGinty, I couldn't wait to get here."

Shifter class. My stomach sank and I picked at my food.

"That poor Dave kid," Wren said. "I hope he's okay."

"Oh, I'm sure he'll be fine," Jas said. "That badger Melinda's healing skills are legendary. She's one of the best there is."

"How do you know so much about the school?" I asked.

"How do you know so little? You said your mom was a shifter and your dad's a mage. You had to have figured there was a chance you'd end up here."

"I'd hoped. But I did my own thing, ya know? I didn't want to get my hopes up in case it didn't happen. Especially with my brother here, if he'd gotten in and not me, that would've sucked."

"I feel ya. Which one's your brother?"

"He's a fourer, but I don't see him in here right now. He's a shifter, like our mom."

"And what's he shift into?" Wren asked.

"A mountain lion."

Jas whistled. "Damn. That's awesome. Beats skunk hands down ten times to Sunday."

"I thought your skunk was pretty cool," I said. "Your shift was the best."

Wren nodded, long brown hair sliding along the front of her shoulders. "By far the best."

Jas tried to suppress her smile. "Well, I figure if I have to be a skunk, then I'll be the best damn one there is. Like a quick draw."

"I'll settle just for shifting, however I get there," I said.

"Maybe not like Dave Bailey though," Wren said with a wince.

"Definitely not like Dave."

"Ah-uh," Jas murmured around a mouthful. "He'll be trying to live that down for a long time."

I smiled. "I liked him. He seemed completely at ease with himself."

"You *like* liked him?" Wren asked, and I had to school myself not to roll my eyes. I'd endured Berry Bramble High well enough, but I had little tolerance for stereotypical teen girl behavior. I had better things to do with my time than waste it mooning over immature boys.

"I just thought he seemed nice is all," I said, trying not to reveal my true feelings on Wren's question.

"What'd you guys think of Beginning Creature History?" I asked, to change the topic.

Jas and Wren groaned at once and I laughed.

"I've never met a boring werewolf before," Jas said. "Hell, I've never even heard of a boring werewolf. They're always so feisty."

"I'm pretty sure Wendell Whittle doesn't have a feisty bone in his body," I said.

"His last name is probably 'Whittle' because he's as plain as a block of wood that needs whittling."

I cringed a bit, but Wren added, "It really was awful. I don't know how I'm going to survive his class. It was the first day and I was already worried about nodding off and snoring or drooling on myself or something in front of the whole class."

I turned to take in Wren. How bizarre. This girl actually thought like me. I didn't think there was anyone as strange as I.

"It's a real danger," Jas was saying. "And we have to read the entire *Compendium of Supernatural Creatures* over the nine terms. Have you seen those books? They're basically encyclopedias. It's gonna suck."

"My dad wrote those books," I said, feeling a bit like a traitor that I'd never bothered to read them before. I couldn't even defend the books; I'd stayed away from them because I'd figured they were boring too.

"Oh," Jas said, and she didn't seem a bit bothered by the fact that she'd essentially insulted my dad's life work. "That's cool. I think."

I stared at her before allowing myself a chuckle. "You know, that's my thought on it too."

"So you haven't read the books?"

"No." I blinked back the discomfort at the admission, then tilted my chin up. "But I'm looking forward to reading them for class." And I was, kind of.

"So am I," Wren said, nodding her head in what appeared to be a sincere gesture. "I can't wait to learn."

"Again, how do the two of you know so little?" Jas asked. "Especially with a dad who wrote the damn *Compendium*, for fuck's sake? You do realize it's like the quintessential authority on the supernatural world, right?"

"Of course I know that," I snapped without meaning to, but Jas didn't appear bothered that I'd reacted more to my annoyance at myself than her. "I really should've read them, because you're right. I don't know jack shit about what to expect, and I totally wish I did."

"Ditto," Wren said. "My parents home-schooled me and all my siblings. They believe in allowing us to discover our own truths and our own sense of self without influence from the outside world."

I thought she was mocking her parents until I saw her placid face.

"So you were raised like a tree-hugging hippie or something?" Jas obviously had no filter to interrupt the brain-mouth path.

Wren smiled. "Something like that. It was actually a nice way to grow up ... in some ways."

"How many siblings do you have?" I asked.

"My mom had an even baker's dozen, as she likes to say."

Jas whistled again. "Dang, girl. Your parents went at it like rabbits. That's a ton. "

"Life was busy, that's for sure."

"Are any of them here?"

"Nope, just me, and I'm number seven and the only shifter so far. Assuming I actually am a shifter if I'm a tree."

"I don't see why not," I said. "You shift into something. That should make you a shifter, right? That's what McGinty said, anyway."

But Jas didn't bother answering. She was following the progress of students entering the dining hall. "Who in blazing hell fire is that?" she said.

I SWIVELED IN MY SEAT ONLY TO IMMEDIATELY WISH I hadn't. I groaned. "Why'd you make me look? Now he's going to think I was checking him out," I said, feeling the silver-haired elfin prince's eyes on my back. "He's already conceited enough as it is."

"Well, that's one man who has every right to be conceited," Jas said. "Look at him."

Yeah, I was trying hard not to, though the pinpricks of Leander's attention continued to sting my back. "He is pretty beautiful, I'll admit it, but let's not get carried away here. His personality is a bit over the top."

"I don't know," Wren said, sounding oddly dreamy. "He seems pretty down to earth to me."

"Well, trust me on this one, he isn't. He acts as if he's already the king of the elves instead of an elfin prince."

"You must be mistaken, this guy is no fucking prince," Jas said.

"Definitely not," Wren said. "He's so strong looking."

I sighed heavily and swiveled on the bench seat. And I accidentally met Leander's gaze, though as soon as I did he moved it and laughed at something some girl who was fawning all over him said.

I huffed and turned right back around. "So arrogant," I muttered. "Strutting in here like he owns the place, girls draped all over him."

"What are you talking about?" Jas said. "He doesn't have any girls on him. Thankfully. Because I'm planning on setting my sights on that fine specimen of a man. Mm-hm."

Wren's face fell, though she attempted to mask her reaction, as if she too had intended to set her sights on Leander. I guessed he had reason to act so arrogant if every girl was tripping over herself to win his attentions. "What, did you miss the busty redhead trying to drape herself all over him?" I asked.

"What?" Jas started. "Not him, you doof. The super hot one with the brown hair and smoldering whiskey eyes."

"The what?" I turned again and groaned the moment my eyes landed on the extent of Leander's entourage. "Dude, gross! The brown-haired one with 'whiskey' eyes is my brother."

"Your brother you say?" Jas wasn't grossed out the way she was supposed to be.

"Hello? My *brother*."

She brushed the thick lock of white hair from her

forehead and tilted her head in a disturbingly flirtatious manner. "So you can introduce me?"

"Wha—? No, I can't introduce you," I whisper screamed. "Not like that, at least."

"What about the one with the ponytail?" Wren asked in a wispy voice. "Do you know him?"

"Who? Boone?"

"Is that his name? Boone," Wren repeated, drawing out the word like a starry-eyed teenybopper. "That's a really nice name."

I shook my head and looked from Wren to Jas, and then back to my brother and his crew. My brother looked up, saw me looking, and smiled.

"Holy. Shit," Jas said. "He's smokin'."

"Again, he's my brother. He and I took baths together when we were kids. He's not hot."

"Naked baths you say?"

"Ew, Jas, no. No, no, no. That's all shades of wrong."

"They're coming this way," Wren said breathily.

"Come to mama," Jas said.

"Jazzzzz," I warned, but all she did was flick her chin-length hair and plaster a winning smile on her face, the kind I hadn't seen before.

Ky sauntered up to the table, with Boone and Leander right behind him, which meant that there were also a handful of girls with them, including the redhead with tentacles for fingers. She was trying really hard to wrap herself around the elfin prince, who did nothing to discourage her—though he also didn't really do anything to return her affections.

"Hey, squirt," Ky said, plopping into the open seat next to me. "How's your first day going?"

"Uh, great." *Thanks for the nickname, jerk,* I added mentally. "It's been interesting so far, that's for sure."

He laughed, a deep, melodic hum, instigating a bizarre chain reaction. Jas giggled, sounding absolutely nothing like the kick-ass shifter girl I'd believed her to be, making Boone chuckle, which made Wren giggle and hide her face when her cheeks flushed at Boone's attention on her. Though he was probably wondering what on earth was going on.

Ky looked at me oddly, and I grimaced. "Ky, these are my new friends, Jas and Wren." I ignored another weird giggle from Jas and said to her and Wren, "And those are Ky's friends, Leander Verion and Boone."

Boone nodded at the girls; the elfin prince stared at me. "You can call me Leo," he said. "I don't stand by formalities here." Even though his perfect posture, immaculate clothing, and powerful eyes suggested otherwise.

"I can tell," I said with a tight, sarcastic smile.

His silver eyes tightened and the girl next to him sidled in closer.

"I see you're busy," I told him with a meaningful look to the ginger. "Don't let us keep you."

"I'm not busy," he said, proving that he was just as self-centered as I thought.

"Come on, *Leo*," the redhead cooed. "Let's go."

Leo's eyes tightened even more when the ginger said his name like that. He removed her hand from his shoulder. I couldn't help but meet his stare.

Ky leaned into my shoulder. "Catch ya later, squirt," he said. "Good luck with roommate assignment." But when he stood and moved to Boone's side, an off-kilter mewl had he and Boone searching for the hair-raising sound.

"Oh no," I whispered, spotting Dave Bailey across the dining hall.

"What the...?" Ky said.

"That's Dave Bailey," I said. "He's in our shifter class."

"So you're in the shifter class?" Ky asked with a grin before Dave mewled again. "Right, not now."

"What's this Dave's deal?" Boone asked. "What exactly is he?"

"He's a bobcat," Wren said, a little too fast. "At least, he's supposed to be a bobcat. Or a boy, I guess, depending. But in our shifter class he was half and half, I'd say."

"Melinda the badger was supposed to have healed him," I said, half rising from my seat, my plate of food fully forgotten. "But something must've gone wrong."

Dave was standing nearly in the middle of the dining hall, all eyes on him. Even several of the trolls had stepped out from the kitchen and serving areas to see what was going on. A third screeching wail ripped through the silence that had descended on the room, and my heart clenched for the likeable boy who was garnering the attention of every single creature there.

"Oh no," he said, wrapping his arms around himself as if he couldn't contain whatever he'd just realized was about to happen next. He pursed his lips

99

shut and a pained expression came over his completely normal boy-face.

"At least Melinda seems to have healed him," I muttered to myself, but like everyone else who surrounded me, I couldn't remove my attention from whatever was about to happen. Because whatever it was, the stricken look on Dave's face promised it was going to be a train wreck.

I moved behind the bench seat and took a step in his direction, but didn't know what to do. I was probably the least qualified to help him.

Dave's entire body contorted, and I hoped he wasn't in as much discomfort as it appeared he might be. Every feature on his face squeezed and his shoulders hunched in on him.

"Oh God," he said, in the manner of one who'd just realized he was about to be sick and couldn't make it to a bathroom in time.

Fur whisked across every visible part of his body, rippling and stretching against his flesh like a funhouse mirror gone horribly wrong. His body writhed this way and that and another strangled caterwaul escaped his body.

"Is he ... shifting?" Ky asked.

"I hope not," Boone said. "That doesn't look right for a shift."

Dave popped his eyes open so wide that they bulged, and as another wave of ... whatever it was ... raced across his body, he collided with the table nearest him. His hands outstretched as he tried to stabilize himself. He knocked two dishes, a glass, and silverware off the table; it all went clattering to the floor in a clanking crash.

A troll with an orange afro marched forward. "That's enough of this, you," he said.

Could he really not see that Dave couldn't control himself?

Dave grunted and groaned and folded in half, clutching at his abdomen and the table. His normal brown eyes flashed a motley color as they began to roll back into his head.

"That's it," Orangesicle said, planting himself directly next to Dave. "Stop this right now."

Dave grimaced and his entire body bent in the opposite direction. Orangesicle moved closer, his beady black eyes just peering over the tabletop. Ignoring the shards of shattered cutlery, he climbed onto the bench seat and placed hands on either side of his hips. Thank God he was wearing an apron.

"Stop whatever you're doing right now or I'll make you."

Another troll sidled up to the scene. "We have rules you must follow in the dining hall, no matter what. Or you have to face the consequences of your disobedience."

"That's precisely correct," Orangesicle said. "Rule number six: No shifting inside the confines of the dining hall. You're clearly breaking that rule."

Bobcat ears popped from the top of Dave's head as his human ears were pulled inward, where they disappeared with a sloshy, sucking sound. His eyes were a *Twilight Zone* mess of human one second, cat the next. A long tail snaked out from above his waist-band and he looked on in horror as his skin rippled, settling neither on human skin nor on fur.

He opened his mouth—whether to scream in pain or defend himself to the trolls, I couldn't tell—and I had seen enough. I marched toward the scene as the second troll with rainbow-colored hair joined Orangesicle on the bench seat. Rainbow brought his hands in front of him and a band of electric sparks jumped between his stubby fingers.

I heard several gasps circle the tables, but I didn't stop. Dave tried to sit on the dining table as he panted in exhaustion, but when he tried to sit on the edge, another wave of whatever—shifter magic gone wrong, I supposed—burst through him.

He yelped and threw his head back as his neck completely shifted into that of a bobcat, but then his human head must have been too heavy for his trans-formed neck, because it started lolling like a dash-board bobblehead going over speed bumps.

Bones shrank with an audible crunch that made me start running toward the boy. I heard footsteps behind me but didn't turn to look. I wasn't sure whether Dave could actually die like this, but I got the distinct feeling that someone had to intervene fast—before he caused permanent damage to himself or the trolls decided to deal with him.

Rainbow tsked. "Rules are meant to be followed," he said, sounding too much like the deranged Rasper the Rabbit who manned the gate, and he let his elec-tric magic fly.

Sparks zinged and Dave's entire body, including the bobcat bits, went rigid, as if he were a statue, if a statute could be electrocuted by a crazy rule-following troll.

"No!" I yelled, and when Rainbow looked up in response to my call, his zapping faltered.

I skidded to a stop next to Dave and reached out for him, not sure what I was going to do beyond getting him away from the trolls.

But a strong hand grasped my shoulders and held me in place. "No," came the voice of the elfin prince as he pressed me against his chest.

"I need to help him," I protested.

"No, you don't," Leander said, his steady voice rumbling through my back.

"Of course I do—"

"Just trust me, will you, Rina?" he said, and I stilled. Even the trolls seemed to study the elfin prince as he leaned me against one of the dining tables and moved toward Dave.

"You will *not* harm this boy," Leander said, in that regal tone I thought I despised. When Rainbow dropped his hands and Orangesicle took a step back from Dave, I loved the imperious edge to his voice. "He hasn't intended to break any rules, so you cannot hold him accountable for rule-breaking when there is no intent to do so."

Leander tilted his gaze down to meet eyes with the trolls'. "You cannot punish where there's been no ill intent. Those are your own laws, the laws of the troll folk."

The tension in the dining hall was thick enough to snap with my bare hands. Dave continued to snarl and squirm and break out in patches of the wrong species. Beyond that, there was no sound.

The elfin prince and the trolls were in a stare-off.

Finally, Rainbow *tsked* as if he were actually disappointed he couldn't punish Dave, then climbed down from the bench seat, mooning the entire dining hall as he did so. Orangesicle followed him moments later, giving me a full shot of round, miniature troll butt.

Leander watched them until they backed up several steps from Dave. When he nodded his approval of their retreat, I swear the trolls' shoulders relaxed in response.

Dave screamed and folded in half so suddenly that whiplash was a very real possibility. I raced toward him, and this time Leander did nothing to push me away. I tried to hold the thrashing Dave, but ended up getting a headbutt to the nose for my efforts.

"Ow. Shit," I said, my eyes smarting at the sudden pain.

"Sawr-ey," Dave said, his voice barely human anymore.

"No more of this," Leander said, waiting for an opening. Ky's arm draped around my shoulders, pulling me close, just as Boone reached around Dave and held him secure in a bear hug from behind. Boone pressed half-Dave, half-bobcat against his wide chest, and Leander placed a palm against his head.

A pulse of silver light exploded from the prince's hand. Like the flash of a nuclear blast, it circled the room in an instant. Dave whimpered for another moment, then collapsed into Boone.

A sigh of relief circled the dining hall and I sank into Ky. He squeezed me closer and I couldn't help but return the squeeze, no matter how many times he'd called me "little" or "squirt" since I'd arrived at the school.

Boone dragged an apparently unconscious Dave over to the bench seat, sat him down with his legs stretched into the aisle, and leaned his back against the table, propping him up like a marionette.

Boone shared meaningful looks first with Leander and then with Ky, before finally landing on me. I met the haunted hazel eyes of the werewolf. There was something soothing about them, as if he'd seen enough horrors and survived them to suggest I could manage the same.

The double doors to the dining hall flew open and Professors McGinty and Quickfoot raced in, with a very harried-looking badger on their heels. The badger took one look at the scene, hiked up skirts that looked like they belonged on *Little House on the Prairie*, and ran toward Dave as fast as a badger on two legs could run.

❧ 10 ❧

MELINDA SKIDDED TO A STOP IN FRONT OF DAVE, McGinty and Quickfoot right on her heels. The badger and gnome moved surprisingly fast, considering their legs were substantially shorter than the shifter's.

"What happened here?" she asked as she slid onto the open seat next to Dave. Her eyes flashed first to Boone, who sat on Dave's other side, propping him up.

"I think a shift came over him when he didn't want it to, but then things didn't go as they should've."

"Meaning?" Melinda's voice was sweet, as if draped in honey, but her tone was focused and efficient.

"Meaning there was something wrong with his shift," Ky said. I wasn't leaning on him anymore, but I didn't leave his side either as we hovered around Dave. My brother's friends and my friends circled closely around, though a hushed murmuring settled across the entire dining hall; everyone was interested in Dave's fate. At least Leander's fan club had moved on to somewhere else.

"He didn't go through the usual steps," Ky continued from above my head. "There was none of the usual blurring, vibrating, or flickering. He appeared to have no control over what was happening."

"It looked painful," I added, garnering a curious look from the badger.

"Hello, dear. You must be Ky's sister. You look just like him."

I scoffed, because Ky and I looked nothing alike. The badger only smiled. "It's the eyes that give it away."

But right away her attention was back on Dave. She rose from her seat and placed paws on his chest and leaned in, sniffing away. "Did the pain of the shift make him pass out?" she asked.

"No," Boone said. "Leander Verion intervened before he could hurt himself. The kid was thrashing into tables when Leander stepped in."

"Hmm, it's a good thing he did." *Sniff, sniff.* The badger smelled his neck, his head, his arms, getting too close to his armpits for comfort, before looking back at Professors McGinty and Quickfoot. "He definitely doesn't smell right. We have a problem. The pathways of his shift are all wrong."

"Oh no. That's not good," McGinty said, while a worried look settled onto Quickfoot's gnome face, or at least the bits that I could see between his bushy beard, mustache, and eyebrows.

"Nope, it sure isn't good," Melinda said. "I don't know how, but the shift pathways are pretty set too. Which means I'm going to have to work hard to reroute them. How long has he been shifting?" she asked no one in particular.

Everyone shrugged and McGinty shook his head.

"He mentioned it in shifter class this morning," I said. How could no one remember? Even then, Dave's shift had been ... memorable. "He said he's only been shifting for four weeks."

"Hmm." Melinda gave a sage nod, as if that meant something. "It's a very good thing you remembered, dear. That will help me."

How? I couldn't imagine. Dave looked beyond repair.

Without taking her eyes from Dave's face, Melinda asked, "How long do I have before he wakes, Leander?"

"Between thirty and forty minutes, I'd say."

How on earth could the elfin prince be so precise? I cast a surreptitious look at him. He met my look but did nothing to suggest the answer I sought. The moment I got some time alone with Ky, I'd have to ask him about the mysterious prince.

"I'll have to work on his head first," Melinda said, almost to herself, though for obvious reasons. Dave's head was fully slumped against his chest, stretching the fur covering the back of his neck taut. "To think I only just managed to right him half an hour ago. That he couldn't keep himself human between then and now suggests our problem is actually quite grave."

"We'll need to alert Sir Lancelot right away," Professor Quickfoot said.

Melinda nodded, her nose twitching. "Call for Nancy, too, while you're at it please."

"Do you want Nancy to get him to the healing wing?" Boone asked.

"Yes. Why?"

"I can carry him there if you want."

Melinda removed a paw from Dave's chest to pat Boone's hand where he held it against Dave's half-furry, half-fleshy arm. "Thank you, dear, it's a kind offer. But I need Nancy to hover him and keep him completely still. I'm worried about how any jostling might instigate more shifting. With how unstable he is, anything could set him off."

I gulped and backed another inch toward Ky behind me.

Professor Quickfoot walked toward a flowerpot in the corner of the dining hall I hadn't noticed before and bent over it, his tall red hat crushed against the wall behind it. With the way his beard was moving, he appeared to be ... talking to it.

"What's he—?" I said.

A flower popped up out of the dirt and shook vibrant blue petals, which reminded me of forget–me-nots if forget-me-nots could, uh, get up and move. The gnome rose, brushing errant specks of dirt from his beard, and headed back toward us. The flower hopped from its pot down to the wooden floor and scooted across it, its roots moving a bit like feet as it apparently headed for the door.

I gawked as the flower spread itself nearly flat along the floor and began to creep beneath the crack of the door like an octopus, squeezing all its bits through impossible spaces. And then the flower was gone.

How would I ever get a good night's sleep in this place if so much of it was alive?—or enchanted, was it?

By the time I was able to get myself to stop staring between the now-empty pot and the crack beneath the large double doors through which the flower had disappeared, things had moved along without me— and Wren apparently, who was the only one sharing a holy-moly look with me.

The din of the dining hall had picked up again, because, I guessed, this was just an everyday occurrence at the Magical Creatures Academy. I gulped. Ky was so gonna get it. He hadn't prepared me for any of this!

Melinda reached into the deep pockets of her apron to extract a small jar of what appeared to be ointment, and was rubbing a thick, orange-glowing gel along Dave's furry bits, especially his neck.

When the smell of it hit me, I scrunched my nose.

"Oh, that's nasty," Jas said.

"It's my experience that the stronger something smells, the better it works." Melinda finished applying the gel stuff and wiped her hands along her flowered apron. "There," she said, "that should help contain things until I can get him back. Where is Nancy anyway? She should be here by now."

"As should one of the fairies," McGinty said, squinting toward the rafters.

I followed his gaze upward just in time to catch Nessa and Fianna materializing with a pair of pops loud enough to set my ears to ringing. Nessa immediately started brushing off her wings, but Fianna's eyes darted around quickly until they landed on our group. Then she dive-bombed right toward us, pulling up at the last possible instant before crashing into Dave.

She landed on the table, and seconds later Nessa crash landed next to her, tumbling a few times before popping up onto her bare feet, wobbling forward.

"Whoa, Nessa," Fianna said, holding out a tiny hand to still her. "Take it easy there."

"What? I'm totally fine. I meant to do that."

"Was Sir Lancelot unable to come?" Quickfoot asked.

"He's otherwise engaged at the moment," Nessa said. "Urgent business. Very urgent business. The shifters and vamps—"

"Are no one's business until Sir Lancelot says they are, *Nessa*." Fianna's tawny eyes seemed to light up as they bore into the fairy with the blue ... well, blue everything but her skin, perhaps.

Nessa winced before catching herself. "What's the problem here?"

"We have a shifter who's out of control," McGinty said. "Melinda says his pathways are all messed up."

"Oh that's bad." Fianna whistled her impression

of how bad it was and flew to land on Melinda's lap, her wings a blur. "*Ew*. What's that smell?"

"It's the finest of magic at work," Melinda said. "Will you please inform our headmaster that this student, a Dave Bailey I believe, will have to be excused from all coursework until I set him right? We can't risk any unknown stressors or factors at this point."

"Maybe he should just go home," Fianna suggested.

Nessa nodded. "He should. So many students are waiting and hoping to be admitted to the school. We should make room for them."

"Fairies," Quickfoot admonished. "You know that's not how it works. The student remains until the school kicks him out. We don't interfere."

Nessa shrugged as if to say, Well, maybe we should interfere.

"There will be enough students kicked out by the end of the first week to make room for new students," McGinty said. "That's the way it always goes—without our meddling." McGinty pulled a McSquinty and narrowed his eyes at the fairies in warning. I wondered why they'd be the headmaster's go-betweens if they couldn't behave.

"Where is Nancy?" Melinda said, her voice rising in impatience.

"Oh!" Nessa said. "Nancy's busy helping Sir Lancelot with the shifter-vampire situation."

Fianna groaned. "The *secret* shifter vampire situation, Nessa. Secret."

Nessa finally had the good graces to flush at her faux-pas before hurrying to change the subject. "You want Nancy to hover the boy to the healing wing? Is that it?"

Melinda nodded. "Yes, I need to treat him immediately."

"In that case…" Nessa said. She puffed her chest. She stood maybe four inches atop the table. "I can magick him there, no prob—"

"No!" Melinda said, before adjusting her tone and her apron. "No, thank you very much, Nessa, but Boone here has already offered to carry the boy, so there's no need."

"I don't mind, honestly." But this time the fairy, with the shockingly blue hair and a lot of skin exposed around her small blue skirt and crop top, narrowed her eyes at the healer. "I'm happy to do it."

Melinda jumped to her feet. "No thank you very much. It's already been handled."

Nessa crossed her arms across her chest and glared while Fianna chuckled.

"You're very important to Sir Lancelot," Melinda continued, obviously settling on diplomacy. "I'm sure he needs you for far more important things."

The trolls Orangesicle and Rainbow finally lost interest in the happenings and disappeared behind the counters. I smiled in relief … and then shrieked.

McGinty, Quickfoot, Melinda, and Leander pinned urgent, sweeping gazes across me. Nessa zoomed to hover in my face. "What is it? Are you all right? I'll help you," the blue fairy said while touching down on my cheek.

I clenched my teeth so as not to swat at her, which I really, really wanted to do. When she leaned in to stretch open one of my eyelids—to better examine my eye, I presumed—I snapped, "Get away from me, you ... fairy."

"Good save," Ky whispered behind me. "Are you okay?"

"I'm fine." I pointed. "It's that. That's not supposed to happen like that, is it?" It couldn't be. Because if it was, this school was all shades of freaky.

The teachers, students, and fairies grouped around Dave swiveled their heads as one. "What? The Magical Moving Mousse?"

"The magical what?"

"The funky smelling orange stuff sliding across the guy's face," Ky said.

"It's supposed to do that?" I said, and immediately cleared my throat to cover up the squeakiness of my voice.

"Of course, dear," Melinda said. "It's containing the shift. It's a temporary measure, certainly, but still very helpful. I always have Magical Moving Mousse with me at all times. You never know when one might need it."

"It looks like it's eating his flesh."

Fianna barked out laughing, high-pitched and highly annoying. I glared at her until I realized she seemed to enjoy the challenge, then I trained my eyes back on the slime skittering around on Dave like a flesh-eating virus. If zombies showed up, I was so out of there. I wouldn't care how great of a reputation the school had.

Melinda flicked another worried glance between Dave and the fairies before saying to Boone, "Thanks for agreeing to carry him for me. Before the fairies arrived."

Boone stood, maintaining a hold on Dave, and nodded knowingly. "Of course. Happy to offer. Any special way I should carry him?"

"Wait," I said, before thinking. "You can't let that moussey stuff touch your skin."

"That's a very good point," Melinda said. "You obviously pay attention to detail. We don't want the gel to attempt to interfere with Boone's shifting ability in any way."

I nodded, though really I'd been worried about Boone getting his flesh eaten and then becoming a zombie.

"Maybe a fireman's hold, Boone. That way, if anything gets on you, it'll be on your clothes."

Boone tossed Dave across his broad back like he was stuffed with feathers.

"Dammmn," Wren said, erupting into pink splotches when I—and Boone—turned to look at her. "Dammit. I mean ... I hope he gets better. He doesn't look so well. I hope he heals. I—"

Jas put a hand on Wren's arm and Wren clamped her mouth shut.

Before Wren or I could say anything else we weren't supposed to, Melinda and Boone blessedly led

locking eyes with Jas.

"I won't if you set me up with your brother."

I groaned. "No way. It's never gonna happen. Don't ask me again."

Jas' face parted in a smile so significant it made the gem dangling at the end of her nose ring jiggle.

"That's not a dare or a challenge," I said.

She only grinned bigger.

"Every student is to report to the main auditorium in Irele Hall," a disembodied voice announced as if it were actually inside my head. I shook my head to push away the discomfort of having a thought that wasn't mine appear in my brain. "Drop whatever you're doing and make your way to the assembly immediately. Sir Lancelot will address you."

"Is that Nessa?" Wren asked.

"It's definitely Nessa," Adalia said. "Her voice has a particular pitch to it. As a fairy, my brain can distinguish the voices of every single fairy alive."

"Yeah, fascinating," Jas said, as she joined the rest of the students in exiting the administration building. "We'll have to come back to get our stuff later," she said to us.

"Definitely." Adalia kept pace with us. "An announcement like this is most uncommon. Sir Lancelot wouldn't call a meeting unless something urgent was happening. I wonder what it might be. Maybe—"

"Do you do any of your thinking inside your head?" Jas asked.

"Jas…" I admonished. Did the shifter not realize

how prickly she was?

"Of course I do," Adalia said, as if Jas had actually asked her a genuine question. It was then that I realized the spell that governed the school was brilliant. Jas and Adalia were the perfect match. Adalia was able to overlook Jas' surly nature, and Adalia would drive Jas insane between now and the end of term.

I caught Wren looking at me and met her broad smile. She was thinking exactly what I was.

Jas slammed through the double doors to Acquaine Hall, rushed down the exterior steps, and picked up the pace until she was nearly speed walking, but still she couldn't lose Adalia. When we finally reached Irele Hall, Adalia—and Wren and I—was right on her heels.

"That's odd, isn't it?" Wren stopped before entering. I followed her line of sight. Leander was walking hurriedly toward Irele Hall, Sir Lancelot and the two fairies flying above him, and Boone and my brother a step behind.

"I wouldn't think it's odd at all," Adalia said. "My prince is exactly the kind of person Sir Lancelot would consult in times of danger and urgency."

"Who said anything about danger?" Jas asked.

"Nessa's announcement did. You have to listen between the lines of what any fairy says to discern the extent of their message."

"Maybe I could if they didn't talk nonstop."

I asked, "What kind of danger?"

"I'm not sure," Adalia said. "But if my prince is

with Sir Lancelot, it must involve the fae in some way. Although I suppose it might involve the entire supernatural community if an alpha's son is with them too. And the mountain lion shifter, he's also powerful."

"He's my brother," I said.

Adalia started and snapped her head toward me. "The mountain lion shifter is your brother?"

I nodded. "Why is that so noteworthy?"

"Because he's hot," Jas said.

Adalia giggled. "He is, but that's not why." When she turned back to me, I glowered at her and Jas. The fairy dropped the twinkly smile. "Don't you know? There are only two mountain lion shifters left in the entire world. Your brother and the head of the Shifter Alliance, or rather, its rogue faction."

I stared at her in shock. "There used to be two more," she said, "a woman who used to be a student here like twenty-some years ago, and the brother of the rogue shifter faction's leader. Now there are only two."

"My brother never told me." Neither had my father. I wondered if it had anything to do with the fact that my mother was the mountain lion shifter who'd graduated from here twenty-five years ago.

"And why is it so significant that they're the last of the mountain lions?" Wren asked.

"I'm not entirely sure," Adalia said, shrugging apologetically. "It might just be because mountain lions are really powerful and we need all the powerful shifters on our side we can get."

"Side? What are you talking about?"

"Didn't you know? Things are a bit crazy right now. There's a divide in our community. Those that want—"

"Come on, girls," Fianna interrupted, zipping up ahead of Leander to shoo us inside. "This is no time to lollygag. Don't make Sir Lancelot wait, especially when he has business as important as this to attend to."

When we didn't move quickly enough, Fianna snapped tiny fingers in our faces. "Are you waiting for paint to dry or something? Move it."

Wren snapped to and pulled one of the double doors open. When Jas filed ahead of me and I turned to do the same, Adalia folded into a deep bow. I looked to see why she was bowing and discovered Leander's eyes on me.

A semblance of a smile quaked across my lips, but he didn't return it. His gray eyes blazed as they met mine and held until Adalia said, "My Prince…"

He nodded at her, shoulder-length silver hair sliding across his straight shoulders, but didn't break my gaze. "After you," he said to me, and I hurried inside ahead of him feeling another set of eyes on me as I moved.

After I claimed a seat in the crowded auditorium next to Wren, I met Ky's gaze. He didn't smile or scowl, but his look was intense. What the hell was going on?

Then Sir Lancelot landed on a tabletop on the dais at the front of the room, and everyone quieted at once.

❧ 12 ❧

NOT EVEN NESSA OR FIANNA DARED INTERRUPT THE silence as everyone stared at the petite owl. His expression was grave, his large yellow eyes drawn due to their intensity. Whatever he was here to announce wasn't good news.

Scanning the audience, he seemed to make eye contact with every single one of us, though I imagined that was impossible. There had to be somewhere between a hundred and a hundred and fifty students, and that didn't count several staff members who'd crammed in here with us. A student had to complete nine semester terms to graduate. However, the number of students who enrolled each year varied, since it was dependent on a spell and not a regular set of admission considerations. I'd estimated our class of oners—as students here during their first term were called—numbered upward of twenty-five students. I had no idea if this was a constant across all the terms, from oners through to niners. I supposed with students getting kicked out at an alarming rate, it couldn't be.

Sir Lancelot cleared his throat. "As you might imagine," he began, his voice loud and clear as it rang through the hushed assembly, "I've called you here to impart some rather important news." As when he'd first addressed our incoming class in this same room, he crossed his wingtips behind his back and began to pace the length of the desk he stood on in a startlingly human manner. Though the owl was small, he dwarfed the two diminutive fairies who stood on either edge of the desk behind him.

"Before I share this troubling news with you, I feel it is my duty to first assure you that you are entirely safe here. There are few safer places in the world, and most of them are fellow satellite schools of the Magical Arts Academy, as this one is."

Schools? Plural? I'd only ever heard of this one. Dad's reclusivity after Mom's death, and Ky's secrecy —not to get my hopes up, perhaps—hadn't done me any favors—though I imagined they would've answered my questions if I'd posed them.

"Our school is well guarded, though I doubt most of you notice the extent of our protection. In the magical realm, we don't take anything for granted, especially not with the amount of unrest that governs our world."

Unrest? I shifted uncomfortably in my seat, noticing that Wren was doing the same.

"While our school is fortunate enough to be nestled inside a mountain, which prevents any potential discovery from non-magical people of the outside world, our location isn't hidden from our magical counterparts, whether they consider themselves friend or foe."

Foe? Why would a school of novice students have enemies?

"The spells in place that protect our school prevent anyone or anything that is not pre-approved from entering. And I assure you there are no finer spells than those that govern the functioning of our school. Lords Mordecai and Albacus of Irele House itself set these spells into place, and I tell you from personal experience that there are no finer or more capable wizards in the world. I've known them for centuries."

Centuries? So the rumors that the owl was more than a thousand years old might actually be true. But how old could these wizards possibly be if they were human? Were they not human? My mind was already reeling and Sir Lancelot hadn't even gotten to the meat of his announcement yet.

The owl scanned his audience once more, meeting eyes in turn with Leander, Boone, and finally my brother, where they sat in the front row. The headmaster came to a stop in the center of the desk that I was beginning to suspect had been positioned there solely for his speeches. Despite his size, the owl emanated power and control.

"Most of you will realize that the world of magical creatures is in turmoil. But this has been the state of affairs for many centuries now. There are factions of shifters, vampires, and other smaller groups of creatures that do not agree with the existence of the Enforcers. Nor do they agree with the purpose of this task force that polices them, protecting the humans from harm and interference from the magical world.

"It is essential that humans not discover our existence, as history has proven time and again that the clashing of our two ways of existence leads only to bloodshed. Those of you more advanced in your studies will recall the Sorcerers for Magical Supremacy and the havoc they wrought in their attempts to expose magic to the world at large. It cannot be allowed to happen." His voice was taut with intensity.

"The job of the Enforcers is crucial to maintaining relative peace in our world. That same job will befall you upon your graduation through your apprenticeship, and after if you choose to remain with the Enforcers. Their mission is more important now than ever before—and more dangerous." He allowed his message to hang in the air around us, where the only sounds to be heard were those of the students shifting in their seats. I cast a quick glance ahead to discover that Leander, Boone, and Ky were some of the few students not to appear unnerved by the length of the owl's reassurances. I assumed the others who appeared calmer were those more advanced in their studies, who had a greater understanding of what was going on in the larger world. Even Jas bit down on her sarcastic commentary and watched the owl with rapt attention.

The owl resumed his pacing. "With those assurances in place and with your understanding of how safeguarded we are within our mountain, our gates secured by Rasper the Rabbit, who allows no one by him that doesn't belong, I announce that the unrest in our supernatural community has reached ... concerning levels."

The entirety of his audience seemed to lean forward as a whole. "You all are aware that the different groups of supernatural creatures have formed their own organizations."

I wasn't exactly aware of it ... of course.

"The shapeshifters have their Shifter Alliance. The vampires have their Undead League, which includes necromancers. There are the wizards and witches who align themselves with the Magical Arts Academy and refer to themselves simply as Mages, and then the creatures that do not fit neatly into any category and loosely call themselves Supernaturals. There are others, of course, as our community is large and varied, and include the fae..." Sir Lancelot tipped his head to Leander. "The werewolves who group themselves separately from the shifters at large..." He looked to Boone with a slight bow of his feathered head. "And others..."

Never had I felt like such a novice, or quite so foolish for not paying enough attention to the world I'd dreamt of becoming part of.

"The powerful Shifter Alliance and the Undead League have long allowed grumblings of discontent for the way the Enforcers monitor them without their consent. Of course, the Enforcers do so because it is the only way to maintain peace and our way of life. We are all subjected to the rules that divide the magical world from its counterpart. Those rumblings have never led to much … until now."

I swallowed around a dry throat.

"A group that calls itself the Voice—of discontent, I presume—has banded shifters, vampires, and other creatures together. So far, there have been no additions of mages. Let's hope that continues, as mages who align themselves with dark magic are fearsome. Likewise, the werewolves have kept themselves separate from the turmoil, as have the fae, as is common for their folk not to become involved in issues such as this."

The pygmy owl grimaced. "The Voice's numbers have grown large enough to warrant concern. Today the organization issued a public threat. The Enforcers are to stand down and accept that they have no authority over shifters, vampires, and the others."

He let his words settle around the auditorium, though I doubt any of us missed that he hadn't mentioned the other half of the threat. What would this Voice do if its terms weren't met?

"You are completely protected here, so there's no need to worry. These are issues that the trained members of our community will address and deal with. Regardless, as all of you will be affected by the ramifications of these actions, I deemed this announcement necessary. In addition, no student will be allowed to leave the school for any reason without my prior approval. The unrest outside of our mountain is too great at the moment. Those who oppose the Voice and its goals are as vocal as the rebels themselves."

The owl spread his wings before bringing them back against his body as if in an unconscious gesture. A tired look settled on the nocturnal creature's face before he whisked it away.

"For those of you oners, or more advanced students as well, who the school rejects and wishes to send home," the owl said, "an escort will be arranged to deliver you home safely. There is no reason for concern at the moment."

Again he scoured our audience, then said, "That is all. You may resume your coursework and activities for today." He turned to speak with his assistants, Fianna and Nessa, his shoulders relaxing by a fraction. But I heard him say, "May the goodness of magic protect us all," before he lowered his voice to a whisper.

I shared an alarmed look with Wren and then searched the audience, which erupted in frantic murmurs. Of all the vampires, I spotted only Professor Damante. I whispered to Jas, "Where're the rest of the vamps?" Sir Lancelot's announcement had made me even more wary of the vampires than usual.

"They would've been initiated by now," Jas said, none of her usual snark present. "Which means they can't be in the daylight anymore."

I gulped. "Does that mean they drink blood now too?"

Jas stared at me, and even Adalia looked a bit

surprised by my question. "Not here they won't," Jas said. "The Menagerie teaches them another way."

"One not all vampires embrace," Adalia added, doing nothing to settle my misgivings.

Just as I was trying to identify which bit of it all had me the most nervous, the entire building shook— walls, floor, the seat I sat in. I gripped the armrests of my chair while Wren yelped and dug fingers into my forearm, scratching my skin since I had my shirt sleeves rolled up. Startled cries circled the room. Sir Lancelot spun back toward us with sharp eyes. Professors McGinty, Damante, and Quickfoot, along with several others who appeared to be professors of other classes, stalked toward the front of the room, gazes crawling across the entirety of the assembly and shooting outside the large windows that lined one wall.

I, too, looked through the windows, but noticed nothing out of the ordinary. From where I sat, all I could make out was a vast, bright blue sky, marred by nothing but a few wispy clouds.

Another rumble shook the hall. Sharp shrieks echoed throughout the room and I sensed Ky's eyes on me. I met them and he half rose from his seat, looking between me and the front of the room, where the professors were congregating.

"Sir Lancelot?" Professor McGinty asked sharply. Every teacher there waited for the owl's reply, their bodies tense.

The owl hesitated, but only for a moment. "We go outside." He cast a look over his shoulder until Fianna flew up to meet him. "The students remain inside until it's clear."

The tiny fairy nodded, as did Nessa, who flew to her other side.

Then McGinty strode to the door to the auditorium, pulled it open, and allowed the owl to fly through ahead of him. The professors filed through the door without a glance back at us.

I had so many questions scrolling through my mind, but none coalesced into a single useful thought.

When the building shook another time, I couldn't contain a startled squeak. I clutched my armrests with an iron grip, though this time the building shook a bit less. Still, there was nothing reassuring about a solid structure, constructed of large bricks, moving beneath you—especially not in the aftermath of Sir Lancelot's warnings.

Ky was halfway up the center aisle to me when girly shrieks erupted along the left side of the room and the wall with the windows. I looked in that direction, seeing several things at once: the feminine cries had come from boys as well as girls; the view through the windows was partially obstructed by a flying shape; and that flying shape resembled what I imagined a dragon might look like.

A dragon. I sank farther down into my seat from the weight of shock.

When I turned again to confirm what I'd seen, clear blue sky filled the windows.

Another rattle settled through the building, making my hair shift across my shoulders. I sought out my brother. Were there dragons … landing on the roof of the hall?

He crouched by my side, prepared to speak, when a small voice swept across the room, filling my head. "All right, everyone!" Fianna called, her wings a blur behind her as she hovered above the spot the owl had occupied. "You heard the boss. Keep calm and in your seats until we direct you otherwise."

Nessa flew next to her, eyes scanning the room as if to spot those with intentions to disobey.

"It's likely only dragons," Fianna said, "so nothing to worry about, really. They wouldn't have been able to get in here unless they're friends of the Menagerie."

I chortled without mirth. Was she kidding? I hadn't seen a single thing not to worry about since crossing through the solid red rock to arrive at the school.

"Dragons have never come to the school before, at least not since I've been here," Ky whispered to me from where he crouched in the aisle.

I nodded absently at the information, vaguely noticing that Boone and Leander appeared to be waiting for my brother. The elfin prince's eyes swept over me, but I didn't react. I was rooted to the spot.

"Remain calm," Fianna continued. "There isn't anything to worry about—"

"Until there's something to worry about," Nessa completed in her usual unhelpful manner.

"Stay with me," Ky said, and I nodded again. My anger at my brother for allowing me to be blindsided by all this had fled. I was going to stick to him like glue if I had any choice in the matter.

When he started down the aisle, I didn't realize he meant for me to follow him until he turned to look over his shoulder at me. I jumped from my seat, displacing Wren's hand, and hastened down the steps.

Nessa shot straight toward me. "And where do you think you're going?"

"I-I'm—"

"She's coming with me," Ky said, injecting raw power into his voice I'd never heard before.

Nessa crossed her arms over her chest and glared. But a look between Ky and his friends finally had her releasing her arms. "Fine, but you watch her like a hawk."

Ky grinned with his entire face. "I'll watch her like a mountain lion stalking its prey."

Power rocketed off my brother, making me realize I hadn't even seen what was right in front of me for what it was.

He grabbed my arm and tugged me along with him, falling into step behind Boone and Leander.

"The rest of them stay," Nessa said.

Ky and I spun. Wren, Jas, and Adalia were intent on following me. Even Jas looked unsettled by the circumstances.

"They're with me," I said, attempting to inject power into my voice as Ky had.

By the way Nessa arched tiny blue eyebrows, I'd managed it to some small degree at least. With a severe scowl of her pink lips that made her pointy ears twitch, the fairy said, "Very well." But then she pinned my brother in a glare. "They're your responsibility out there."

He nodded, and the fairy harrumphed. Then Ky pulled me through the open door.

❧ 13 ❧

THE MOMENT I WALKED OUTSIDE, MY STEP FALTERED. Oh, they were dragons all right. Gigantic creatures with enormous wings, tails that passed for weapons, and teeth and claws that could rip a person to shreds in a few messy seconds.

Ky tugged on my arm to set me in motion again, my friends traipsing behind me with equally hesitant steps. I craned my neck back to take in the ferocious animals atop the roof. There were two dragons … and a rider atop each one.

My heart thumped in my chest. How on earth did a person dare to ride such a beast? One of the dragons, the larger one, thumped its tail against the roof— undoubtedly rattling the windows in their panes within the auditorium. The dragon was a sparkling scarlet; its scales reflected the sunlight as if they were glittering rubies.

"Set down here," Sir Lancelot called up to the

roof while gesturing with a wingtip to the open grassy field in front of Irele Hall.

The rider who sat atop the crimson dragon gave a curt nod and bent to speak to the dragon. Moments later, the dragon spread its wings so that they blotted out the sun, swept them downward, then lunged up, its hulking body jerking as it gained enough altitude to swing around and land in the appointed area.

I couldn't take my eyes from the sight, nor from the girl who appeared to be at most a few years older than I sitting behind the dragon's neck, her legs' strength alone holding her atop the beast. Her hair was flaming red, as bright as the dragon she rode. I discovered myself as mesmerized by her as the creature she straddled.

I registered that the second dragon also took off from the roof, but I watched the blood-red dragon swing in for a smooth descent, landing immediately next to Sir Lancelot, who swallowed a muffled yelp and flapped his wings in hurried motions to get out of the dragon's way.

While the red-haired girl leaned forward across the dragon's neck to speak into its ear, Sir Lancelot addressed Professor McGinty: "Conal, will you kindly allow me to perch upon your shoulder? This dragon hasn't learned any better manners since I last saw him, which means I trust him even less than I did when we last met, and I barely trusted him then."

"Of course," McGinty said, tilting his head out of the way to make room for the headmaster on his shoulder.

Sir Lancelot took his place on the shifter professor, then immediately crossed wings in front of his plumed chest, glaring at the scarlet dragon. I would've smiled at the comical sight if not for the terror that continued to drum through my veins.

The slightly smaller sapphire dragon set down behind the red one, where its rider waited with a straight back. My eyes scanned the two beasts, trying to decide which of the two was the more magnificent. As light reflected off it, the blue one sparkled just as much as the red. It was every fantastical storybook I'd ever read about dragons combined into one scene.

"Wow," I muttered to myself, finally remembering Ky, his friends, and the host of Menagerie staff that waited with us. I attempted to pull myself together a bit, smoothing my hair and my features, before looking over at them.

Ky and Leander were looking at me already, but only Leander's slate eyes danced with amusement. Was he laughing at me? I settled my mouth into clearly *un*amused lines.

He smirked and rustled his wings behind him where they pressed against his back, magically emerging from his school uniform shirt without any tearing. Oh, he was definitely laughing at me. I swallowed a growl and turned my attention back to the important business among us.

The flaming-haired girl slid down her dragon's side and leapt once she reached his belly—the gap between it and the ground was nearly large enough to fit me. She landed on the grass with light feet before tumbling into a roll to break her momentum, then popped straight up to her feet and didn't even break stride as she made her way to the owl.

I blinked, wondering where this girl had come from. Not only did she ride dragons, but she was apparently amazing. She flicked a long braid across the thick leather padding of her flying suit and cast a quick amber glance at my friends and me.

The dragons' eyes were more mesmerizing than hers, with their vertical slits and deceivingly lazy look, but only barely.

When she neared Sir Lancelot, the red dragon took several steps toward her, though the blue one didn't move from its position.

The owl cocked what would have been a hip in a person and glared at the dragon some more.

"Sir Lancelot," the girl said with a respectful bow of her head.

"Destine." The owl flicked quick eyes to her before returning them to the dragon. "I see that Humbert is as much a brute as ever."

The girl chuckled. "Only when you're around. He likes you."

The owl scoffed. "Likes me? Oh no. He likes to terrorize me is what he likes to do."

The girl smiled. "Maybe. He doesn't do it to anyone else."

I finally looked to my friends with raised eyebrows. Did what? I was obviously missing something … yet again. But none of my new friends, not even the ever attentive Adalia, responded to my unspoken question.

They appeared as entranced by the supposedly mythical beasts as I was. I didn't think even Dad's *Compendium* mentioned them as anything beyond creatures of legend, now believed extinct.

Destine scanned the small crowd amassed before her. "I bring urgent news."

The owl pinned his attention on her. "I imagine so to enter the Menagerie in this manner. It's never been done before."

"Regardless, with the news I have to deliver, it may happen again soon. We've entered different times."

Maybe the girl wasn't close to my age, though she looked it—if I ignored the weight of responsibility that seemed to burden her. She sure spoke more formally than any friend I'd ever had.

"My news is for your ears alone," she continued. "The Master was very clear on that point."

Sir Lancelot studied the red dragon behind him—Humbert, apparently. "Very well. But that dragon of yours will have to behave."

"I don't fool myself into believing he's mine, Sir Lancelot, but I will ask him to behave just the same." She stalked back to her dragon with sure steps.

"Are you sure it's a good idea?" Professor McGinty asked the owl.

"I'm entirely sure it *isn't* a good idea to remain alone with the dragon who's had it out for me for more than a hundred years, Conal, but I don't see any way around it. We need to learn what the Master has deemed so urgent. He isn't one to exaggerate."

"If you're sure..." Professor Quickfoot said. His

bushy gray eyebrows low on his brow, he peered at the dragon with suspicious eyes. I suspected the dragon was fully aware of the trouble he was causing and enjoying it … assuming dragons were capable of such behavior. Since Humbert was a bloody dragon, when dragons weren't supposed to exist, I could only suppose.

"Thank you for your concern, Burl," the owl said. "I'll be fine, though I'd appreciate it if you waited for me just beyond the clearing, in case I need your assistance."

The gnome gave a sharp nod that tipped his tall red hat low, glared at the dragon, who appeared to preen under the attention, and backed away toward the copse of trees that edged the clearing, never taking his eyes off the one dragon. He didn't once flick his attention to the blue dragon.

Sir Lancelot alighted from McGinty's shoulder to land softly on the ground right in front of the large shifter teacher.

"Signal in any way if you need us," McGinty said and, like the gnome, moved away with backward paces, not a single glance toward his destination.

"Come on," my brother said to me, gripping my arm again and leading me away. Wren, Jas, and Adalia shadowed my steps, eyes wide and sparkling. Even a fairy like Adalia seemed unable to get over the presence of dragons, though Leander didn't appear surprised.

I counted thirteen professors huddled at the edge of the clearing with us, every single one of them in protective stances, ready to charge at any moment. A smallish woman, slighter even than Jas, emitted a deep and constant growl that had the hairs across the nape of my neck prickling. Though she was tiny, no doubt she was fierce. That dragon had better behave … though what could any of them do against a creature as large as a building?

"Don't worry," Ky whispered, leaning close to my ear. "There's more to them than meets the eye."

I couldn't tell whether he meant the professors or the dragons. I suspected it was true in both cases. While the Menagerie was selective and exclusive in its student body to an extreme, it was even more so when it came to its instructors. Everything about the school was tailored to put out the best and most skilled Enforcers this world had ever seen.

Despite his fluffy feathers, the owl appeared more insignificant than usual standing on the ground, barely taller than a flower. But the scarlet dragon remained put as his rider met Sir Lancelot in the middle of the clearing. When she began to speak, even the trees leaned forward, trying to pick up a hint as to what was so important. Destine's hands were tense at her sides, unless they were moving in sharp punctuations of whatever she was saying.

The girl, lean and obviously strong beneath her leather suit that could pass for that of a high-speed motorcycle rider, crouched next to the owl, who peered up at her, unblinking while she spoke.

The teachers amassed around me tensed and shifted as a group, waiting, watching … until finally

Destine rose, gave the headmaster a sharp yet quick bow, and turned back toward her dragon. When she was several paces from Humbert, she broke into a sprint.

Three feet from the dragon's bulk, she leapt off one foot, latched onto the beast's front leg, and scaled up it with the dexterity of an ape. By the time she slid a leg across the creature's neck again, I was certain every single one of us, including Leander, must be in awe of her. I snuck a glance toward him only to discover he looked cool as a cucumber. My scoff drew his attention to me. Again with that slight curl of his lips that suggested he was mocking me.

I snapped my head back to the dragon in time to see Destine lean forward over his neck another time, then straighten and pat him along its length. The dragon stretched his wings wide with a jerking movement, swooping them low … grazing the owl along his exposed chest with the tip of a scarlet-scaled wing.

The dragon's ruby wingtip didn't push hard—just enough to tip the bird and set him off balance.

But the petite professor behind us growled viciously, and she, McGinty, and several of the others raced toward the headmaster.

Humbert swept his wings down and leapt into the sky as if he'd never intended harm at all. The way Destine pursed her lips and bunched her eyebrows low suggested otherwise.

By the time we reached the owl, he was spluttering, something I hadn't believed the composed headmaster could do. "Every time," he rattled. "Every single time the brute tries something like this. For a hundred years! Each time, he pushes me. He knows I know what he's doing, and it makes him do it all the more. No respect. A beast with such appalling manners should be … caged or something!" He flapped his wings around him in a fluster.

"Are you unharmed, Sir Lancelot?" asked the woman professor, who had to be some kind of ferocious shapeshifter, while Professor Quickfoot, the shortest among the teachers, crowded closer.

"Did he hurt you at all?" Professor McGinty asked in a dangerous tone, shooting menacing glances at the red dragon flying away, the blue dragon lifting off in its shadow.

Only Professor Damante and Leander appeared unaffected by the display, though I wasn't sure vampires ever got upset. Rumor had it they rarely became unsettled, and the older they were, the less likely it was. To be a teacher, Damante had to be more experienced than his peers. And Leander, well, little seemed to ruffle the fae prince, though something simmered inside him. I just didn't understand what had his eyes alight.

Sir Lancelot continued his harried spluttering and wing swinging until Destine called from fifty or sixty feet in the air. "Sorry about that! I guess he still has a long way to go in learning his manners."

Destine was too far to make out her eyes, but from the tinge of her voice I suspected she didn't mind her dragon's mischief all that much.

The headmaster narrowed his eyes. Apparently

he'd noticed Destine's lack of concern too. "I'm absolutely fine," he grumbled to the rest of us. He brushed his wings along his body. "Better than before, really, because now I've decided that Humbert has some payback coming. After a century, he's pushed me too far. He'll pay next time."

The vampire professor's lips curved into a dangerous smile, though the mirth didn't light his dead eyes. "If you need any help, do let me know. Vengeance is one of my specialties."

I shivered at the thought and edged closer to Ky, who wrapped an arm around my shoulders, something he rarely did before we arrived at the school.

"I'll keep that in mind, Lorenzo, thank you," Sir Lancelot said. When he turned and craned his neck all the way up to take the crowd of us in, he added, "The Master's message was for me alone. However, I do need to confer with the entirety of my staff. Burl, please ask Fianna and Nessa to dismiss the students, and then meet us in my library office. The rest of you professors, please join me now."

He fixed Leander, Boone, and my brother in his sights. "Students, please remain behind for now." He looked to my friends and me before moving back to the three men. "I'll call on the three of you once I'm ready. I'll need to know what your fathers think about this." From the way he said it, it seemed like he might have included all of their fathers—including Ky's— our father.

What would Dad offer the situation as a magical

historian? Did Sir Lancelot even know Dad? I'd never heard Dad mention the headmaster.

No explanations were forthcoming. Sir Lancelot flew onto McGinty's waiting shoulder and pointed the way ahead with a wing as if he were an infantry commander. The professors marched behind him while the gnome ran on stubby legs in the opposite direction.

As soon as they were out of earshot, Jas said to my brother, "He would've allowed you to come along if we weren't here."

"Probably." Ky was watching the teachers' progress with squinted eyes. I recognized the look; it meant he was thinking hard. Eventually, he felt my gaze on his face and turned to look at me and then Jas, who blushed and smiled at him, making me swallow a groan. "It doesn't matter. We'll find out what's going on soon enough."

Leander and Boone nodded, seemingly just as pensive as my brother.

I was pretty sure it wasn't my place, but I'd learned my lesson from not asking questions before. If I didn't ask, for sure we wouldn't find out. "What did the letter from your father say?" I asked Leander.

He snapped his gaze on me, the one that was like liquid mercury, and Adalia gasped. "Rina, he's a *prince* of the *elves*," she whispered.

I squirmed against Ky, wishing I hadn't said a thing. "Sorry," I said, worried that somehow wasn't enough for whatever transgression I'd committed.

Leander held my eyes even though I was desperate

to look away. Wren whimpered behind me. "My father, the king of the elves, wishes me to return home," he finally said in a tone worthy of a palace or castle or whatever it was the elves had. With that thought, I realized how improper it probably was to address him the way I had. Though there was no way I was curtsying to him as Adalia did.

"It's what my father wants too," Boone said, his shoulders wide enough to bear the weight of an entire race of creatures—the werewolves. "He says it isn't safe here anymore."

I gulped, and Wren took another step toward my back.

Leander smiled, but it came off more as a grimace. "It isn't safe anywhere anymore."

"So why do your fathers want you to go home, then?" I squeaked.

Ky answered: "Because there they have the entirety of their people to protect them."

I nodded slowly. "So ... you'll be going, then?" I asked Leander, wondering why the thought was a heavy one, before taking in the friendly face of Boone.

Boone grinned, exposing teeth, and his friendliness vanished. There before us was a werewolf capable of taking on any foe, and well positioned to do so. "I'm not going anywhere. I've never backed down from a fight before. Not planning on starting anytime soon."

I nodded and gulped as I addressed the prince. "And you?"

"My father can do without me. I'm the second

prince, not the heir. My brother will serve him while I remain here."

Adalia gave a sharp intake of breath. I guessed no one defied the king's orders, even when they were under the guise of requests.

I wanted to look away from the prince; his eyes were intense—too intense. But I couldn't break his stare. Perhaps this was one of his powers.

"And what if something happens to you while you're here?" I whispered.

"Nothing will happen to any of us here. I'll make sure of it."

How, I had no idea. From the curious look Ky was giving Leander and me, I suspected he didn't either.

According to Sir Lancelot, we were entirely safe within the school grounds and there was nothing to concern ourselves with. The Enforcers would deal with this rebellion and set things right once more.

So then why was my stomach churning, and my limbs twitchy?

Ky squeezed my shoulders before dropping my arm. "Come on, squirt. Lots to do around here."

I heard every word he wasn't saying. My brother was worried too.

14

"COME ON, HURRY IT UP. I DON'T WANT TO BE LATE TO class," Jas said, gesturing at the mostly uneaten pancake on my plate. It was drenched in maple syrup —the real stuff—and I still couldn't get myself to finish it.

"Since when do you care about following rules?" I grumbled.

"Since I get to learn cool shit when I do."

I pouted and pushed bites of pancake around my plate.

"Oh, it's not all that bad, is it?" Wren asked, scooting closer on the bench seat she shared with me in the dining hall. "You're making progress."

I chortled. "Only if by 'progress' you mean something other than my understanding of the word. I've been at this for weeks and I still haven't shifted. I haven't even managed a Dave Bailey shift." I shot an apologetic smile at the boy sitting on the other side of Jas. "No offense, Dave."

"None taken," he said, speaking while he chewed. The misfit had gravitated toward us lately. "Shifting is tough, no doubt about it. I still haven't gotten it down."

I blinked at him and didn't say a thing at first. He sure hadn't mastered shifting. But even he had progressed from a train-wreck of a shift to a four-car pile-up. I set my fork down and pushed my plate away from me, giving up on eating. "But you're getting better. And you're a shifter, for sure. Me…?" I shrugged. "I don't think even McGinty knows what to make of me."

"Don't you worry about what McShifty thinks," Jas said, employing her latest nickname for the teacher. "You've heard him. He's not giving up on you."

"But maybe he wants to and is too hardheaded to do it."

"He's definitely hardheaded, but he isn't giving up, because you're at the school for a reason. You know that."

I nodded absently at Jas. I'd heard the argument like a thousand times since our second shifter class, when I'd failed to blur, vibrate, or flicker. I hadn't even managed to botch my first shift as splendidly as Dave had. I'd stood in front of my peers and done absolutely nothing. "Maybe I'll get kicked out soon."

Saying that was voicing my deepest fear, though there was a secret part of me that wished I'd have to leave the school. If I wasn't here, then I couldn't show up for Basic Shifting 101 every single day to fail anew.

Jas, who'd proven she wasn't one to mince words,

shrugged. "Maybe you will. But until then, what've you got to lose?"

"My pride."

She barked with laughter, setting the hanging gem in her nose ring to swinging. "Girl, I'm pretty sure you have none of that left at this point."

"Don't mind her," Wren said softly, rubbing a hand across my back. "She's just grumpy."

"I'm not grumpy," Jas said right away, and Dave, Wren, and I all chuckled at that. "What? I'm not. Just because you get to live with nice roommates and I have to put up with the most unbearable roommate there is doesn't make me grumpy."

"You're a grumpster. Own it," Dave said around another bite.

Wren giggled. "Adalia is like the sweetest girl on this campus."

Jas threw her hands in the air. "Exactly! It's more than a normal girl like me can bear."

I eyed her. "Are you really suggesting you're normal?"

She scowled at me and flicked the white stripe in her hair back across her head. "*Hmnh.* There's nothing wrong with normal."

I laughed. "Since when?"

"Since she's too hardheaded herself to admit she put her foot in her mouth," Dave said. When Jas shot him a death stare, he scooted down the bench seat away from her and put his hands up. "Hey, I just call it like I see it."

"Yeah, yeah," Jas said. "Let's go see how your shift

goes this time." Mischief sparkled in her eyes, but I cringed at the bite in her tone. Jas didn't seem to understand the difference between sarcastic and mean. Or maybe she did and just didn't care.

"I'm sure your shift will go great this time," Wren said in an upbeat tone that tried to make up for Jas.

Dave rubbed at his disheveled brown hair. "I really hope so. I'm tired of smelling like that Magical Moving Mousse stuff."

"*Reeking*, you mean," Jas said.

"Jas," Wren and I admonished in tandem.

"What? What'd I say?" She genuinely didn't appear to realize.

Instead of answering her, I pushed up from the table. "Come on. Let's get this over with."

"It could go well," Wren said in a sweet voice.

I nodded. It *could* … if my shifter magic, or whatever it was I had, deigned to show up for once.

"Pick up your plates," said a voice that put Jas' biting tone to shame.

"We were just about to," Jas said to the troll who'd tried to punish Dave for his out-of-control shift.

"'Just about to' doesn't cut it around here," Orangesicle said. "We're not your servants, you know. We work here because we want to. We get good rewards for working here, but that doesn't mean we have to clean up after you." The troll's fluorescent orange fro crested the tabletop as he glared up at us with dark, pupil-less eyes.

"We're cleaning up our plates right now," Wren said, purposefully not peering over the table to make eye contact. We'd long ago learned to agree with the trolls, no matter what they said—at least all of us but Jas had. She still couldn't resist the occasional jab, though the rest of us steered clear of her when she chose to poke the disgruntled creatures. Whether I remained at the school or not, I still wanted to live.

"Be sure that you do," Orangesicle snapped, before sauntering off to harass the next table of students. All four of us turned to take in his retreat.

"I just can't get over it," I said as I stared at the troll's round little bum on full display. "Why don't they wear real clothes under their aprons?"

Jas shrugged. "Why do trolls do anything they do? They probably do it to defy kitchen health standards or some shit."

Dave said, "I happen to agree with the kind of health code that prevents those handling the food from being bare-ass naked."

Wren and I nodded. "Totally," I said. But what we thought didn't matter much at the Magical Creatures Academy, where more things remained a mystery than their opposite. In the time since Destine's sudden arrival atop Humbert and the influx of talking missives, I still hadn't learned exactly what was going on. Jas, Wren, and I, often with the added input of Dave and Adalia, had discussed the issue of the Voice and the gravity of the threat it posed more times than I cared to count. But we made little headway, and even Ky was more tight-lipped than usual, resisting most of my prodding to get information.

As Dave pulled open the door to the dining hall—

after delivering our plates to the dish-washing depository, of course—I gave the flowerpots next to the door a wary look. They appeared entirely like normal flowers, but like most things on this campus tucked deep within Thunder Mountain, things were almost guaranteed to be far more than they seemed on the surface.

The flowers didn't move or scuttle as I followed Jas out the door, but a sense of foreboding settled deep in the pit of my stomach, where I knew from experience it would simmer all day long.

৩১৯৩

Professor McGinty had taken to having me follow right after Dave when he shifted during class. I suspected it was to encourage me with the lowest standard of all the oner shifters. McGinty usually started the class with Jas, whose shift was the smoothest I'd seen, beyond Ky's.

"You'll do great, lass," the shifter teacher said, just as he did every morning, five days a week, in some variation or another. "You have it in you, for sure. Just don't hold back."

I wasn't exactly sure what it was that I had in me, but whatever it was, the school considered it sufficient to warrant an invitation to study here. I grabbed hold of that one fact and held on to it for dear life. Even Dave had been able to shift—more or less—right away. With how much trouble I'd had to summon even the slightest blur to my form, I feared I was in for a rocky ride once I finally managed to make headway on a shift.

I peered around the large room inside Bundry Hall, which looked more like a wrestling practice area than a classroom with all the padding that covered much of the walls and floor. Half the dozen or so students were bored already, having seen me stand in front of them for weeks with nothing to show for my efforts. The other half, including my friends, smiled encouragement, probably feeling sorry for me.

I rubbed clammy palms in front of me and nodded my head. "All right. Here I go."

"Remember, all you have to do is be open to your own particular kind of magic," McGinty said. "Don't worry about picturing what kind of shifter you are, because you don't know. Just because your mother was and your brother is a mountain lion doesn't mean you'll be one."

I nodded again. I realized all this. I supposed the professor didn't know what else to say to me after so many attempts.

"Every shifter is as unique as their DNA," he continued. "You could be anything, so don't limit yourself by trying to picture a mountain lion."

"Got it," I said, ready to be done with my next bungled attempt already.

"Just let loose." The teacher threw his arms to the side and swayed as if he were one of Sedona's New Agers experiencing unseen music. "Let your magic flow through you. Let it spark and ignite you. Allow it to tingle your senses."

Jas' muffled laughter reached me from the back of the large room, but I refused to react.

"I'm ready," I asserted again and clenched my eyes shut.

Whispers circled the gymnasium. "Silence," McGinty said, and even though the professor was easygoing, power vibrated in his voice, and everyone hushed immediately.

I nodded again, the gesture on repeat, trying to convince myself it wasn't ludicrous to try this for the umpteenth time, that something could still happen and I could still reveal myself as a shifter.

I went through the motions regardless. I'd witnessed enough of the Menagerie's magic to be amazed by the spell that governed so many of its functions. It was massive in scope, incredible, the kind that didn't make a big mistake. I simply had to have some kind of creature magic to be here.

But when I managed to relax myself and empty my mind of its expectations, there was still nothing.

I bit down on my frustration and waited, ignoring the occasional snickering that echoed across the room. Once I'd waited long enough to even grow bored myself, and just as I was about to give up—again—I summoned a bit more determination.

I had to do this. There was no way around it. I'd be standing here until the term was over if I didn't get it done.

I spread awareness throughout my body and along my limbs, until I either sensed a tingling in my extremities … or I was making it up.

I waited for the tingling to evolve into something greater, but it didn't.

So I did exactly what McGinty had warned me not to do and what Jas claimed she never did to prompt a shift: I pictured the edges of my body blurring in my mind. I pulled up an image of myself as if I were another student watching me now and envisioned the edges of my body growing hazy; my forearms and legs, exposed beneath my school uniform, losing their crisp definition; the shirt, skirt, and my Converse going blurry; the individual strands of my hair blending into a single sheet of amber. I pictured my wide copper eyes, plump lips, and the round face they rested on, all fading into the background of me, whatever I really was.

I pictured the details of myself and then released them, where they retreated to the background, allowing my true essence to take the spotlight.

What was my true essence? What made me a worthy candidate for the Menagerie?

I disregarded every one of McGinty's instructions and felt along my body for the spirit of a mountain lion. No matter how the genetics of shapeshifters were passed on, it was still possible I might be a mountain lion shifter like my family, though the odds were low. I was nearly as likely to be a skunk like Jas or a bobcat like Dave—on his good shifting days when he managed to more or less pull the change off.

But even as I whisked my awareness throughout my body, I didn't sense mountain lion. Nor did I sense any other shifter. I experienced only myself ... failing at this yet again.

I'd already decided to surrender to another mark on my failed attempts scorecard when I gave the energy tingling through my limbs one last push—almost like a thanks-for-nothing kick of frustration.

That's when a chorus of gasps reached into my awareness, removed from the here and now. Gasps. Those were different than the snickers and the gossiping whispers.

Within my consciousness, I traced along the contours of my body, searching for the cause of their surprise. But I discovered only more tingling, a vivid energy that traveled the length of my form. Nothing shifter-like. And definitely nothing mountain lion-like. It was no more than if I'd allowed my limbs to fall asleep from inactivity.

After one last search for progress, I sighed heavily and opened my eyes.

Every single set of eyes in that room was trained on me. Professor McGinty's were the widest.

I scanned the students for clues as to what was going on, but the only hint I received was Jas' maniacal grin.

"What's...?" I whispered, but trailed off when I looked down at my hands and arms. They weren't blurred in the least, so epic fail there, but they were ... what?

Glowing like I was a one-woman neon sign...

"What the...?" I took in the honey-colored energy —magic?—that covered my body in a steady hum. It was like the badger Melinda's Magical Moving Mousse ... only it wasn't.

I flashed the widest set of eyes of all at our teacher. "What's going on?"

He shook his head, his thick hair flinging all over the place. "I have no earthly idea." Then his face split into a wide grin, lighting his saucer eyes. "But I know I like it, lass."

I wasn't sure what to think, much less if I liked this latest development. I was covered in glowing, magical goop. But one thing was clear, I'd finally given the class something to talk about. There wasn't a bored expression to split among them.

Basic Shifting class devolved into a buzzing frenzy while shock took root inside me.

I turned my hands this way and that, and the honey-looking stuff moved along with them. I poked the finger of one hand against the palm of the other, but I didn't feel anything unusual.

Still, there was no doubt about it. I was currently rocking unusual. This wasn't normal. But who wanted to be normal anyway?

✢ 15 ✣

PROFESSOR MCGINTY DISMISSED THE CLASS A FEW minutes early, to a chorus of groans. Finally I'd given my classmates an interesting show and they didn't appreciate missing the after-party. But the intensity of our professor didn't brook any arguments, and they filed out quickly, glancing over their shoulders at me.

I'd clung to Jas and Wren like lifelines since arriving at the school, which was so entirely unfamiliar to me. Now I was all alone with the shifter professor, who was tense all over, his muscles bunched as if ready to pounce, his walnut-brown eyes blazing.

"I have no idea what this is," he said, but he actually sounded excited at the thought. "This is … well, it isn't shifter magic, that's for sure." His eyes sharpened, losing a bit of their burn. "Unless it's some kind of new shifter magic. I suppose that's entirely possible. It has to happen sometime, right? Why not with you?"

I'd never heard McGinty ramble like this before, and he wasn't finished yet. His hands moved in a flurry of excited gesturing. "You're definitely a magical creature of some sort. And while there's no real guarantee you're a shifter, it's the most probable thing. You're not a vamp, and what else would you be? Shifting definitely runs in the blood, just not any type of creature…"

I knew all this, and he must realize I did. I had the feeling he wasn't speaking for my benefit anymore.

He waved thick, fluttering fingers at me. "This is magic, without a doubt. Maybe it's your own flavor of shifter magic, lass. Like maybe you can actually manipulate your shifter magic beyond shifting shape!" His deep voice, with a hint of the Isles to it, rose in a crescendo. "This could be … oh my…" He turned in place looking toward the now-empty doorway to our classroom.

"I have to call Sir Lancelot. He needs to be informed right away. There's no one more knowledgeable about magical history than he. If anyone can figure out what's going on with you, it's him."

Then McGinty ran toward the mostly blank brick wall that enclosed one side of the vast room. "Where is it?" he mumbled as he raced back and forth in front of the wall. I'd never seen this side of the gruff and usually more-or-less composed teacher. His behavior reminded me of a child hopped up on sugar.

I allowed my hands to drop to my sides as I took a few hesitant steps toward the professor and the wall that captivated him. It was plain brick on the inside, free of any of the stucco finish that coated the interior spaces of most of the school.

McGinty pressed so close to the wall that I wondered if he'd scrape his nose against the rough brick. "It's got to be here. I know it is." He finally ceased his frantic scurrying back and forth and stopped in one place, moving his head in a constant sweep that made me dizzy just looking at him.

"Uh, Professor...?" I tried. Maybe whatever had happened to me was causing some effect in him? We had no idea what the glowy goop really was. It wasn't out of the question to wonder if it might be unhinging my normally collected professor.

"Not now, Rina. We need to get Sir Lancelot here while this is still happening. He needs to see it with his own eyes to give us the best diagnosis."

"Then ... shall I go fetch him?" I didn't really know where to find him since I'd heard him mention several different office locations, but surely I could figure it out before my instructor lost it entirely.

When McGinty didn't answer right away, I said, "Professor...?"

"Ah!" he exclaimed. "There. I knew it had to be here." He moved right against the wall and pressed a hand to a brick that looked just like all the other bricks surrounding it. "They made the mark very hard to find. I'll bet it was a fairy who did it. Those tinkly lasses are always making trouble, never taking things seriously enough."

I took a step back and sat to wait. I didn't understand, but that wasn't new. I studied the glow that coated me while McGinty inched his face right next to the appointed brick and called out—loudly. "This is

Conal. I need Sir Lancelot to come to the shifter practice room in Bundry Hall right away. Immediately. He'll want to see this." He pulled back, then pressed his lips so close to the brick that he appeared to be speaking against the rough surface. "Tell him to hurry."

He pressed a hand to the brick and it flashed in a quick wave of light, as if the brick had a moment of glory as a disco ball with a beam of light sweeping across it. The rainbow of sparkling brightness extinguished as rapidly as it'd arrived, and then … nothing.

"Hmm," the professor said. "That should do it. I guess. I've never had to use Brick Bams before." He turned giddy eyes on me and scanned the length of my body. "Good. The reaction is still there. We need it to hold until Sir Lancelot gets here. Make sure you hold it."

"I'll do my best, but I don't even know what I'm doing to cause it in the first place. Which makes it pretty difficult to hold it."

"Wow. Even stranger." But he said it like it was a good thing, like my unusual behavior had just made his month.

A pop exploded in the large gymnasium space, but this time I didn't flinch. I'd grown accustomed to the sound that followed the appearance of the small messenger fairies.

"What is it?" Fianna asked right away, even as she flew in a circle trying to identify where her attention should go.

"It's that." Professor McGinty pointed at me.

Despite his enthusiasm, I couldn't help but feel like a specimen caged in a zoo.

I stood still while Fianna zoomed toward me at alarming speeds. Her wings were tiny; she zipped around as fast as a hummingbird. She got right in my face, flew to my temple, and poked at me with her small finger.

"Hey!" I said and stepped back from her. She only flew along with my retreat.

"What the kinackle is it?"

I momentarily dropped my offense at her rude behavior while I pondered what "kinackle" might mean. When she poked me again, I flicked a hand in her direction.

"Stop poking me," I snapped while she flew out of reach. But she didn't withdraw any farther. Her tiny crimson eyebrows were arched in surprise.

Fianna brought hands to her hips and scrunched up her small face. "I've never seen anything like it. You're right, Conal, Sir Lancelot needs to see this, and right away." Though she was right up in my business, she addressed the teacher and not me. "I'll go fetch him with haste."

"I don't know if I can hold it—" I started, but was interrupted by another loud pop, signaling that Fianna didn't much care what I had to say.

"Good," McGinty said. "That means Sir Lancelot will actually come now. The fairies act as go-betweens more than I'd like. But the headmaster is a busy man —owl, I mean."

I understood his mistake. The owl behaved more like a man than many men I knew.

The professor started to circle me, whistling his amazement as he went. "Lass, I knew you'd surprise me. I just had a feeling about you."

I narrowed my eyes at him. Did he really? It was easy to say in hindsight, though he'd certainly encouraged me plenty...

Double pops rang through the cavernous space, and right away Fianna zoomed toward me with Nessa in her wake. "See?" Fianna said to the slightly smaller, blue fairy. "Isn't it wild?"

"Totally." Nessa's eyes were as wide as they got, making them approximately the size of a pin head. "I can't wait to see what Sir Lancelot thinks." It appeared to be the overarching sentiment. By now, I couldn't wait to hear his pronouncement either.

"When will he arrive?" McGinty asked.

"He was right behind me," Nessa said. "After Fianna told us what was happening, he took off immediately."

As if on cue, the owl swooped through the open door. When his yellow eyes landed on me, they expanded to impossible proportions, even for an owl. He glided straight toward me, stopping only once he was a few feet from me and I'd stumbled backward in anticipation of a collision.

He landed on the floor in front of me. "Lady Rina Nelle Mont," he said in that sophisticated voice of his. "I must say, you do surprise."

McGinty ran to the owl's side. "Do you know what it is? Have you ever seen something like it before?"

"Not exactly, no." He craned his neck all the way back to look at me. I met his gaze and forced myself not to smile at the little owl who, from here, appeared to be all head.

"Conal," Sir Lancelot said, "might I alight on your shoulder so I can better study the pupil?"

"Always." McGinty crouched and bared his shoulder for the owl, whose large talons dug into the shifter's shirt.

"Move me as close as you can," Sir Lancelot said, uncaring that I was obviously uncomfortable as the two creatures invaded my personal space. To make things worse, the two fairies were zooming around me like mosquitoes.

"Nessa," the owl said without moving his stare from me, "please go fetch Kylan and bring him here, post-haste."

"And the two boys who are always with him?" she asked.

"Yes, them. Bring them too if they wish."

"Right away," Nessa said with a pop that was so near my ears that a ringing vibrated through my eardrums.

I frowned. I didn't want Leander to see me like this. I didn't suppose I wanted Boone to see me like this either.

When Sir Lancelot finally took in my expression, he asked, "What is it, Rina?"

Startled to be on the spot under so much scrutiny,

I shrugged as if I weren't half as affected as I was. Though my stomach churned and I was sure my cheeks must be flushing beneath my glow, I worked to pretend I wasn't freaked out. "I don't understand what's ... happening to me."

The pygmy owl's feathered face broke into a kind smile, or at least what I interpreted as a smile; with all the feathers and the beak, it was difficult to tell. "It's magic, Rina. You've begun to access your magic."

I arched my eyebrows in question.

"Sir Lancelot receives regular updates on all the students here," McGinty said.

Ah. So the owl was aware of my repeated failures.

"But," I said, "is this shifter magic? None of the other students had anything like this happen. They just ... shifted into their animal or tree or whatever it was. Well, more or less shifted. At least they were working toward that direction." Great, now I was rambling from my nerves. "I didn't blur or anything before this happened. I didn't even vibrate or flicker. None of that. How can this be shifter magic?"

Sir Lancelot peered at me with wisdom shining through his eyes. I discovered myself holding my breath while anticipating his answer. "Magic manifests in all sorts of different ways, for magic is incredibly personal. It's as specific to us as are our personalities. While this isn't common to shifter magic..." He gestured to me with an outstretched wing. "There's no doubt that you're some kind of magical creature, likely a shifter. There's been no mistake. The Academy Spell doesn't make mistakes. You belong here, not at the Magical Arts Academy."

My shoulders relaxed infinitesimally beneath their luminosity. How had he known I'd been worried about that?

"Though it does seem like the kind of magic that only mages can access," he mused, tilting a wingtip back to rub at his chin. "If I weren't so certain you belonged here, I myself might wonder if you'd fit better in the Magical Arts Academy, where powers like this aren't entirely unheard of."

My shoulders tensed all over again. Did I belong here or didn't I? Was I a shifter or not?

The owl tilted his head in the opposite direction, continuing to study me. I experienced his gaze, along with McGinty and Fianna's, like a touch caressing my skin. "Your father is a wizard, correct?" he asked.

I nodded, gulping visibly.

"He's the scholar who put together the tomes of the *Compendium of Supernatural Creatures*."

I wasn't sure if it was a question or not, but I nodded again anyway.

"Hmm," the owl said as Nessa popped into the room right next to my head, setting my ears to ringing anew. No one else seemed bothered by the volume.

"They're coming," Nessa said, and the owl nodded, not moving his stare from me.

"It's as if you've inherited your father's magic instead of your mother's. Though it can't be possible. The Academy Spell wouldn't have invited you here if that were the case."

"Are you saying she has the magic of a witch?" McGinty asked, sounding entirely incredulous.

"Well, the more I study the magic that surrounds her, the more I'm led to that conclusion. It doesn't look like any shifter magic I've ever seen in my nearly one thousand years of life."

One thousand years? The owl had really lived for a millennium? Well, shit. My heart rate sped up for a few moments while I absorbed what it might mean for an owl as astute as this one to have never seen any magic exactly like this goop in all the time he'd lived. Every conclusion I arrived at wasn't particularly good or anywhere near as exciting as the expression McGinty continued to wear on his bearded face.

"It doesn't look like any witch magic I've ever seen either, however," he continued, "but it's far more similar."

"She can't be both a witch *and* a creature, of any sort," McGinty said.

"No, she can't," the owl said. "That's what makes this all the more intriguing."

"Intriguing" was one way to look at it…

A sudden urge overcame me to run or bawl or do something to discharge the rocky, wild energy brewing inside me. I fidgeted, shifting from foot to foot, clenching and unclenching my goop-coated fingers.

"It appears the girl isn't doing anything to maintain the manifestation of powers either," Fianna said. I glared at her third person reference of me. She happily ignored me; she was good at that.

"It does appear that way," Sir Lancelot said. "As if

this were so natural to her that she doesn't even have to think of it to make it happen."

But that wasn't entirely true. I'd pictured myself starting to shift and then this happened when I sent my attention to my body.

"Is my sister okay?" Ky's voice called ahead of his entry into the gym. A second later, he and Leander ran through the open door, Boone no more than a step behind them.

I tamped the reaction to shy away from Leander's sweeping look, only because there was no place to hide from his scrutiny. His moonlight eyes rolled like mercury again as he took me in, from top to bottom and back again.

I didn't smile at him. I did nothing. I was frozen to the spot, and I no longer understood all that rooted me to it.

Ky was the first to overcome his shock enough to sprint across the space to stand beside McGinty, and Sir Lancelot on his shoulder.

"Wha-what is this? What happened?" My usually composed brother sounded as confused and concerned as I was. When McGinty explained for me, Ky's eyebrows lowered across his bright eyes and he frowned. I didn't think he even realized he was doing it.

"It can't be Dad's magic. There has to be some other explanation."

"And if there isn't?" Leander said. Though the elfin prince stood behind my brother and McGinty, his ardent gaze drew me to him like a magnet.

"Then we might be looking at the first dual mage-shifter in all of recorded magical history," Sir Lancelot said.

Boone whistled. I was so rocked by the headmaster's suggestion that my glowy goop retreated, leaving behind goose-pimpled skin and a whirlwind of nameless emotions.

❧ 16 ❧

THE STARES DIDN'T ABATE WITH THE DISAPPEARANCE OF the neon-sign effect. If anything, they intensified while those gathered before me attempted to figure out how I'd made the glowing goop recede with as little apparent effort as I'd made it appear in the first place.

Despite all the attention sweeping across my body, I experienced Leander's gaze separately from that of the others, its own independent trail that left my skin almost feverish.

I refused to allow myself to do it, but my eyes operated of their own accord, lifting to meet the rolling mercury of the prince's gaze. His eyes held mine unabashedly, and with an intensity I didn't understand, though my entire body flushed in response.

I couldn't even blink, staring into the graceful planes of his face, the arrogance I attributed to him wholly forgotten. All the reasons I'd settled on for why

I didn't like the man seemed to have vanished. I struggled to remember them, aware it wasn't smart to allow myself to go down the path his eyes seemed to suggest was open to me. Could Leander Verion, prince of the elves, actually be ... interested in me?

Or maybe I was reading too much into things and he was simply gawking at my freakish display along with the rest of them? That had to be it. Of course it was. He was one of my brother's best friends. Older than I and far more experienced. He was royalty, for goodness' sake. I was a girl with an uncertain future, and a father who resented her for the death of her mother.

I finally blinked, and when I opened my eyes again the burn of his stare remained, along with my confusion.

Neither of us shifted until Ky gave us pointed looks. Then Leander whisked his silver hair behind his shoulders with grace and nonchalance, pushing his wings out a bit before pulling them in against his back once more.

At the insistent press of Ky's gaze, I finally tore my attention from Leander. Ky was glaring at me. Immediately, I offered him a look that asked *What did I do?* fully injected with my innocence, but he didn't react as I'd hoped. He crossed his arms and scowled. I had no doubt he and I were going to have words later.

Even Boone looked curiously between all of us ... until an entirely different sort of tension permeated the air of the gymnasium.

"What is it, Sir Lancelot?" McGinty asked in response to the way the owl had gone rigid.

"Shh, not now," the owl snapped. His lack of manners suggested that whatever was happening was bad. The owl valued etiquette more than anyone I'd ever met.

Professor McGinty appeared to have drawn the same conclusion as I. He pressed his lips shut and held his head still so as not to disturb the owl perched next to it, but his eyes frantically roamed the open space we occupied.

My breath froze in my chest while we waited for Sir Lancelot to explain himself. I wasn't sure what he was reacting to, but I did sense something ... out of place ... off. Though it was also possible that I only thought that due to the owl's suggestion.

He gasped, an odd, strangled wheeze through his beak.

"What? What is it?" Nessa asked, despite how the owl had admonished McGinty for interrupting.

"There's ... oh my goodness, I think there's some-one, something, preparing to harm the school." His voice was panicked, causing my heart to race wildly within my chest.

Fianna hurried to say, "But that can't be, can it? No one can enter the school unless the Academy Spell approves them. Not without setting off the alarms."

"The headmaster is connected to the Menagerie in ways of his own," Nessa said, her words a rush of distress.

"The Academy Spell would've alerted us if we

were in danger," Fianna said. "We'd know about it before—"

Alarms cut through the air, slicing it like the swords of our enemies, whoever they were.

Fianna and Nessa's diminutive mouths dropped open.

The alarms chimed in open space, just like the bell that announced the start and end of classes. Only these weren't the sounds of pleasant bells. It was like a foghorn, blasting out a clear warning of danger.

A rush of energy sped through me, urging me to respond to the caution. To run, to hide, to do something, anything at all. But I hadn't the faintest idea what to do.

I ran to Ky's side. Despite the occasional differences my brother and I had, we'd been each other's safety nets since we were old enough to realize Dad wasn't always capable of being there for us. He plopped an arm around my shoulders right away, pulling me against him.

"What do you need us to do?" Boone asked the headmaster.

The owl shook his head a few times, as if to clear it, and finally he said, "I'm not entirely sure, Boone. I can't get a clear sense of the threat we're under. I'll need to go see it before organizing us."

"Go see it? Does that mean you know where the threat is coming from?" McGinty asked.

"As you know, all the creatures at this school are connected to me during their tenure here. I sense Rasper the Rabbit's distress." But his voice didn't contain urgency, only sadness. That could only mean ... I swallowed thickly and leaned closer to Ky, feeling foolish for having entertained silly notions of the elfin prince while the killer rabbit at the gate was apparently under some kind of attack.

I suspected everyone there interpreted Sir Lancelot's reaction in the same way. The faces surrounding me settled into lines of grim determination.

"Fianna and Nessa, your job is to secure the students," Sir Lancelot said.

"Where do you want them?" Fianna asked.

"Take them to the dining hall and enclose everyone there. No one's to leave without permission. Tell the trolls to prepare for battle."

My eyes grew wide. Whoa! This was ... crazy. Battle? At a school?

But the fairies only nodded. "And what of the more advanced students?" Fianna asked.

"Yes, I suppose it might become necessary." The owl grimaced as much as a bird could. "Any fourers and up should do what they can to prepare themselves. I hope we won't need to call on them."

"Better safe than sorry," Nessa said meekly.

"Exactly. Fourers and up are to remain put until told otherwise. We'll assume that this is just some mistake until such time as it becomes clear that it isn't."

"Is that all?" Fianna asked over the blaring horns. They grated against my nerves, making me twitchy

with the need to get out from under their warning …
and away from whatever threatened us.

"Yes—wait, no, it isn't. Get Melinda and Nancy in
the dining hall as well. All other staff should meet me
at the gate. Let's hope a temporary healing wing won't
be needed, but until I can better gauge things, let's
prepare. Hopefully we'll end up considering this a
drill." His smile didn't fool me; he didn't believe it for
a second. Whatever he was sensing through his
connectedness to the school and its staff and students
was telling him more than he was revealing to us.

"The fledgling vampires won't be able to travel to
the hall. Get word to Professors Damante and Vabu to
remain in the dormitory with all the vampire students,
of all levels, and to guard them. Have them send word
if they need help."

Fianna and Nessa fluttered in front of the owl.

"That's it. Now move," the owl commanded in a
tone I'd never heard him use before. "Keep alert to
any further instructions I might send."

The fairies tilted their bright heads in curt nods,
then blinked out of the practice room. The siren was
so loud their pops were barely audible.

"What do you want me to do?" McGinty asked.

"You come with me. We're going to see Rasper the
Rabbit, or whatever's left of him."

Shock stilled my features into inexpressiveness.
See? I knew the owl was aware of more than he let on.

"The gate has been breached," Sir Lancelot said
in a monotone that suggested he was working to keep
emotion from his voice.

McGinty kept it together. The only thing that gave away his reaction was a subtle twitching of one eyelid. "What about sending an SOS to the Enforcers?"

"Absolutely. You'll help me with that too." The owl nodded solemnly before turning to the rest of us. "Boone, Leander, Ky, I'd instruct you to join the others in the dining hall, but I won't waste my breath. You realize we aren't prepared for something like this, and you'll do all you can to protect the school."

Three succinct nods punctuated his statement. My brother was as stubborn as they came; apparently, so were his friends.

"Escort Rina to the dining hall, then join me at the gates. If necessary, we'll put out the call for the advanced students to join us once we arrive."

"Got it," Boone said.

"Watch your backs," the owl said, sweeping a look between Boone and Leander, and finally to my brother. "Or your fathers will have my head to display on their mantel."

But why would he look to my brother?

"Let's go, Conal," the owl said. "To the gate." He pointed ahead with a sagging wing. Dread and foreboding seeped into his voice. The chill of it lingered in my bones long after the shifter professor jetted through the door with a hand against the owl to steady him.

Ky, Boone, and Leander spared a second to stare at each other. I watched as their shoulders tensed, their backs straightened, and resolve infused every one of their movements.

"Let's go kick some ass," Boone said.

I hoped they still planned to deliver me to the dining hall before they did any ass kicking.

Ky shifted his grip to my hand and led me from Bundry Hall at a fast run. I clutched at him as I realized he'd be heading into danger while I cowered in the dining hall. With him out of sight, I wouldn't know what was happening to him until it was too late.

My breath came quickly, and it had nothing to do with our running. I'd never hyperventilated before, but I suspected this was the beginning of it. What if something happened to Ky?

I snapped myself from that thought. No, it wouldn't—it couldn't. I needed my brother, more than I cared to admit.

I wouldn't let anything happen to him.

Yeah, right, Rina. And how are you going to manage that, exactly? You don't even know how to shift, and you apparently have weird-ass magic. I shut the nagging voice in my head the hell up, and focused only on trailing Ky. Things would go our way. They just had to.

THINGS DIDN'T GO OUR WAY, NOT EVEN A LITTLE BIT. The shifter practice classroom was very nearly on the opposite end of campus from the pearly gates the killer rabbit guarded. But as soon as we exited the building, two very large men rounded the corner and spotted us.

Boone and Leander froze, and Ky shoved me behind his back. McGinty and Sir Lancelot were out of sight, disappeared in the opposite direction I presumed.

An open grassy area of about fifty feet separated us from the men, but the distance seemed like too little regardless. When two other men, equally vicious-looking, though perhaps a fraction smaller, tore around the corner behind the original two, the distance that separated us shrank even further.

Seconds beat out as if they were minutes, marked by the thumping pulse bouncing along my throat.

These men meant us harm. I didn't think they had it out for us in particular—why would they?—though the air of menace they projected didn't discriminate. For whatever reason, they'd deemed us their enemy.

Leander took a step forward that separated him from Boone and Ky—and myself tucked behind him. "What is your purpose here?" the elf asked in a voice that carried evident authority. I imagined it was the tone of royalty.

One of the large men laughed, a full body sound, though it didn't carry any mirth. "What is our purpose here, he asks." The other large man beside him, who looked a bit like the first, laughed loudly enough, but his eyes were jumpy. The smaller men behind them chuckled too.

Then the man, who was apparently their ringleader, addressed Leander. "We just want to be left alone," he said, though an air of menace coated the simple statement. "Nothing more."

"For someone who claims to want to be left alone, you're certainly going about it in an odd way."

Leander held his head high, revealing no fear, though he was thinner and leaner than any of the men—most people would be.

Boone stepped next to Leander and crossed his arms across his chest, biceps bulging. Boone was as large as the ringleader and his second, but Boone was the son of an alpha, next to inherit control of the Northwestern Werewolf Pack.

"What? We're not doing anything," the ringleader said, his smirk revealing that he thought his mocking words were hilarious.

Leander just smiled at the man, and for the first time I caught a glimpse of the elfin prince's power. His eyes narrowed as if he were in on a secret the men who'd infiltrated our school weren't aware of. Boone reacted only by deepening his scowl. Ky spread his legs wider and crossed his arms too, perhaps to attempt to further block me from the men's sight.

"If you're not doing anything, then leave," Boone bit out, his voice gruff, as if his wolf were close to the surface.

"We would, see, if y'all would leave us alone." Ringleader took a single step forward and the three men surrounding me visibly tensed. Even Leander couldn't disguise his readiness for attack.

"We're not doing anything to you," Ky called. "Go back where you came from."

"But y'are. You and the Enforcers act like you're all high and mighty and can tell me and my brother here, and the rest of us shifters, what to do." He took another step toward us. "When ya can't. See, we're stronger than you. And we're here to prove it."

"It sounds like your beef is with the Enforcers, not us," Boone said.

Ringleader's second shook his head, and when he spoke even his voice was similar to his brother's. "You guys will be Enforcers soon enough."

"So you'd punish us for perceived future sins?" Leander asked.

Ringleader advanced toward us a bit more, and the three men behind him shadowed his steps. "We warned y'all. We even issued a public statement announcing what would happen if we weren't taken seriously."

The second nodded. "We can't be blamed if you didn't take us seriously."

"We didn't do anything," Ky said. "We're just students." But I suspected Ky would be saying something entirely different if I weren't there.

Ringleader and his second shrugged, mirroring each other's gestures. I peeked at them from around Ky's shoulder. There was something eerie to the similarities between the brothers.

"What's the difference?" Ringleader said. "Whether we kill you now, or we kill you later, the result is the same."

My heart skipped a beat at his casual use of "kill."

The men advanced toward us again and I realized with a start that they were stalking us in the same manner that predators in the wild stalk their prey. They weren't here to talk or resolve a thing. It didn't matter that their blame was misplaced, we were their target. And it was four massive men against three students—albeit advanced ones—and me, who didn't count as even half a student as far as skill went.

The blaring of the school's sirens finally came to an end, leaving the silence that erupted in its wake ringing. When Ringleader spoke next, his voice softer in the absence of the alarm, his words were somehow even more menacing. "You can make this easy on yourselves and just surrender."

"And what happens if we surrender?" Ky asked, moving toward his friends while sliding me along behind him. Again, I suspected he wouldn't be asking this question if I weren't caught in this situation with him.

The second man said, "If you surrender, we won't hurt ya." I might've believed the sincerity of the smile that followed—maybe. But I sure as hell didn't believe the gleam in the eyes of the other men surrounding him.

They meant to kill us, no matter what we did.

As if Leander, Boone, and Ky had arrived at that exact same conclusion, the three friends lined up together with me directly behind them.

They flexed their muscles. Leander cracked his neck by tilting his head to either side. He stretched his wings so that I had to scramble out of their way, before returning them to their place against his back.

"If shit goes down," Ky whispered to the elfin prince, "you get her out of here."

I didn't think the men across the way could hear

Ky. Leander looked to my brother, then to me behind them, and shook his head. "You're crazy if you think I'm leaving you and Boone to take them on alone."

"You have to do this for me, man."

Leander froze rigidly for a few moments before shaking his head again. "You can't ask me to abandon you guys in a fight. You need me. There are four of them."

"What I need is for you to keep my sister safe."

"Why me then?"

"Because you can fly, and we can't."

Leander waggled his jaw back and forth as he considered. When he started shaking his head again, Ky said, "Come on, man. Please. I need to trust that no matter what, my sister will be okay."

The elf's nostrils flared and his eyes swirled with displeasure, but finally he gave one, succinct nod.

I wouldn't die here today; Leander would whisk me away first, flying high above the fight ... leaving my brother and Boone to die alone.

Hell, no. I opened my mouth to protest when the sounds of cracking bones circled the grassy knoll. And it wasn't just Boone and Ky, the men across the way were clearly shifters too.

Their fierce animal counterparts were about to make an appearance. And I would be a useless weight dragging my brother and his friends down.

I shook my head. No, this wasn't how it was going to go down. I wouldn't allow it.

I gritted my teeth and squeezed my eyes shut, reaching for something—anything—that would help.

The sound of shifting bodies became so loud that the crackling and popping infiltrated my brain, my every thought.

I reached for the sounds as if they were somehow my salvation. It made no damn sense, but I went with what I felt, instinct perhaps. I knew of nothing better to do.

17

THE FOUR LARGE MEN ACROSS THE WAY HUNCHED over, curling in on themselves, while their bodies contorted every which way. The snapping and crackling that accompanied their movements was loud enough to make a damn Rice Krispies commercial. Their faces scrunched up in grimaces that left me no doubt their shifts were brutally painful.

But why? Why would they do it this way and leave themselves vulnerable for attack after the faster, relatively painless, shifts of Boone and my brother? Even Dave Bailey didn't look to be suffering as much as this when he botched his shifts.

Boone and Ky's bodies advanced through the usual blurring, vibrating, and flickering, only they moved through the stages so rapidly that the transitions merged into one seamless progression. They made Jas' shift seem remedial in comparison.

In less than thirty seconds, Boone had transformed into an enormous wolf, whose head reached beyond my waist. His fur was a thick, mottled gray; his paws were as wide as saucers. But my attention settled on the sharp rows of teeth he bared at our would-be attackers, and the way his eyes, yellower than usual, revealed no fear.

No wonder his father, the werewolf alpha, considered Boone worthy of inheriting his role in leading the pack. Boone was intimidating as all get out. Thank goodness he was on our side.

Then my attention drifted to Ky, who'd also completed his shift and was stalking toward the four vulnerable shifters. Unlike Boone, Ky's mountain lion was average-sized for the animal. That still made him as tall as Boone's wolf, but broader. The mountain lion had thick shoulders and hips, and moved with the grace and strength of a wild creature accustomed to killing for survival.

The subdued whimpers of pain the four men emitted were beginning to subside. Ky flicked a look over his shoulder at me and I gasped. His animal was stunning, all efficient and agile lines of muscle. Ky's mountain lion was a kingly beast among men. Those copper eyes of his glowed while they ensured that Leander stood next to me, prepared to intervene should he deem it necessary.

Then Ky flicked those copper orbs to Boone, who'd already moved next to him. Some silent understanding passed between them, and in the next instant they were charging toward the other shifters, whose transformations were nearly complete.

Ky and Boone covered the distance in seconds,

making me feel like I was watching the nature channel with the way their legs moved so quickly that their paws hardly kicked up dirt, merely grazing the grassy knoll as they sped toward our self-appointed enemies.

Ringleader snapped into the body of a ... m-mountain lion. How was that possible? The chances of him sharing a form with Ky were next to nothing.

Yet my eyes couldn't deny the terrifying sight. That meant that Ringleader and Ky would be evenly matched, the win coming down to who wanted it more, who caught the other one unaware.

Ky leapt at Ringleader's lion when the animal turned and caught his first clear sight of Ky. Ring-leader froze, eyes the color of a cold and heartless desert widening in evident shock.

That second of hesitation was enough to give Ky the upper hand. My brother swiped a giant paw at the other lion, sending his head spinning, his body chasing after the momentum to ease the blow.

Boone lunged for one of the other animals, taking on a bear who was significantly larger than Boone's wolf, but incomplete. A few glimpses of the previous humanity of the shape's owner continued to undulate across the bear's body as the final pieces of the animal clicked into place. That gave Boone a momentary advantage.

He lurched for the bear's throat with wide-open jaws. As he latched onto the bear's throat and shook his head back and forth with a few vicious shakes, I stepped back ... and into Leander's firm body behind me. His hands moved to my shoulders while I reeled at the intensity of Boone's attack. I hadn't expected him to take the kill shot like that. A bear, for goodness' sake. In the wild, wolves wouldn't attack the stronger bear.

The bear released a strangled roar. Boone clamped his jaws around the bear's throat and didn't release it even as the creature thrashed its head, attempting to rise to his hind legs to force the wolf to break his hold.

But Boone held on … until the other shifter fully completed his shift and raced to the bear's aid. The other shifter had become a wolf nearly as tall and as powerful-looking as Boone. And the rusty-colored wolf lunged at Boone's hind legs with a wide jaw, lips tight, teeth bared in a deadly snarl.

I gasped in terror and shuffled backward, only then remembering that my back was already pressed against Leander's body.

He circled his hands around my waist and pulled me flush against him, leaning to whisper against my ear, "It'll be all right."

But how could he possibly know that? Boone was about to get mauled by another wolf, and if that bear's shifter magic managed to heal him enough to turn the tide and make the fight two against one...

No, things weren't going to be all right. Not unless Leander and I did something to even the odds.

"We have to help," I said, trying to untangle myself from his grasp.

He gently wrapped his arms more fully around me. "We have to wait. I promised Ky."

"Well, Ky won't be worried about whether or not

you keep your promise to him if he's dead." My voice welled with my panic.

Too much was happening at once. Ringleader's second was off to the side, prowling around Ky and Ringleader. My brother appeared to be evenly matched, and although Ringleader had a bloody gash across his neck and the front of one shoulder, it didn't appear to bother him—at least not enough to tip the fight.

But the other shifter, his second, I couldn't be certain. Was he … was he another mountain lion? It seemed impossible when the shape was so rare. Only two living mountain lions existed in the entire world. Wasn't that what someone had said? One of the messenger fairies, perhaps? I couldn't remember, but I recalled the fact perfectly. Yet here were Ky and Ringleader … and that made two. Which meant his second couldn't be one, though he looked a lot like one, if not for the way the curves of his face were off, and the slope of his shoulders and hips were wrong for a mountain lion.

His tail was no more than a stub when it should have been long and erect. His entire body was highly asymmetrical. It was like whoever made this shapeshifter was drunk when fashioning him, deviating from the usual perfection of the animal's design in enough ways to ensure he'd never be the strongest or fastest.

In the wild, the second's animal would be dead, victim to the process of natural selection.

Ky and Ringleader circled each other, teeth bared

in a constant series of low growls and snarls, while the warped quasi-lion prowled around their circle with a slight limp on both sides of his body.

My brother darted quick glances across his shoulder at Quasi while trying to keep his sights on Ringleader at all times. Poor Ky! It was too much.

"If you won't let me do something to help," I said to Leander behind me, of course without a single idea of what I might do to help even if he agreed, "isn't there someone we can call to help?" We were at the finest school for shapeshifters and magical creatures in the world, after all. The vamps wouldn't be of any use in the sunshine, but the rest of them could assist. "Sir Lancelot mentioned the advanced students. Can we get them?" I asked.

"There isn't time." At the regret in the elfin prince's voice, I remembered that these were his best friends fighting to protect us, and that he would've certainly thought of everything he could to ensure their survival. He was far more familiar with the work-ings of the school, but also with the gravity of the threat. Not only was he a fourth term student of the Menagerie, he was also a prince of the fae—and a well informed one based on the frequency of the chatty letters that arrived for him.

"The fight will be over in minutes," Leander said.

"Then can you do something to help them?" I asked, turning to look at him over my shoulder, anxious at having to remove my gaze from the fights even for an instant. A second was all it would take for a claw to gouge the wrong area, for teeth to pierce vulnerable flesh.

Already we were on borrowed time. Growls and a constant, steady hum of deep animal voices had me flinching and crawling in my skin.

But Leander met my eyes with a steadiness I couldn't grasp just then. The silver of his eyes didn't roll as it usually did when he looked at me; it swayed with the calm of a sea, wild storms brewing below the surface. "If you're asking if my powers are great enough to help them, the answer is yes."

He was talking too slowly. He needed to move now, now, now!

I studied him and then didn't bother suggesting it. I could read the message in his gaze. He'd given himself over to fate.

"But if I risk myself, there's always that chance that I will be taken down," he said. "And if I'm taken down, there will be no one left to save you."

I was speaking before he'd properly completed his last word. "I don't care. Help them. I can run away or something so they can't get to me and you can keep your promise to Ky."

"There's no guarantee you'll get away, and then I'll have failed my friend."

The friend who was potentially dying as we had this conversation. "I'll run away right now and go as fast as I can, straight to the dining hall. I won't go anywhere else." I promised, even though I wasn't entirely sure I could leave Ky while he fought for his life. What if the worst happened and I left him to die without me?

But Leander appeared to actually be considering my proposal, so I shut my mouth and broadcast a repeated cycle of *pleases* through my eyes. I turned to face him entirely, shifting my weight from foot to foot.

He looked to his friends, then me again, and finally shook his head, his silver hair skimming his shoulders, which sagged beneath the weight of his decision. "I'm sorry, Rina, I really am. But if I let you go, you might run into any number of situations like this one. And on your own, you wouldn't make it out."

"So fly me away now, take me to the dining hall, and come right back. I'll raise the alarm once I get in there."

The look he gave me told me what he wouldn't speak in words. There wasn't enough time for all that, and if we left, my brother and Boone—and Leander's best friends—might suffer the worst of fates without anyone who loved them to witness it and share the burden.

It was only then that I realized that what Ky had asked of Leander was a greater sacrifice for the prince than risking his own life in the fight. The elf battled his every instinct in his desire to protect me. The evidence was everywhere now that I understood what I was looking at—the way his entire body vibrated with a subtle, potent intensity. His urge was to race forward and fight. Yet he stood stolidly, his hands wrapped around me, protecting that which was more important to his friend than his own life.

My eyes blurred at the recognition of the extent of Ky's sacrifice. I whipped around to face front again, wishing I could beat time.

The bear was down but not dead yet, thrashing against the grass, which was quickly flooding in a pool of its blood. Its eyes were gradually becoming glassy.

Boone fought the rust-colored wolf in close combat. Both wolves exhibited bleeding gashes across their sides, though none appeared necessarily deadly. Theirs was a lethal dance of lunges, swipes of claws and teeth, and then a quick retreat before the other wolf could retaliate. Without knowing more about Boone, I couldn't guess who would come out victorious beyond the strength of my desire that it be he.

And Ky … he kept jerking quick glances behind him at the quasi creature that worked to keep hidden from his sight. Though far less of a threat than the fully empowered mountain lion across from him, Quasi was a threat regardless, especially since my brother was outnumbered and—I swallowed a lump as big as an apricot—wounded.

Blood dripped down the front of my brother's leg, staining his sandy-colored fur in red. The lion across from him was injured too. A foot-long slice down his side dripped blood as steadily as my brother's wound.

Neither mountain lion revealed the depth of his injury. Their movements continued to be smooth, calculated, and vicious. Each of the two animals hunched their heads down into their shoulders, seeking the opening that would allow them to end the other.

With the way Quasi was darting constant looks between my brother and his, I figured he was waiting for some kind of sign from Ringleader.

"We don't have much time," I said to no one.

Leander moved his fingers in soothing circles around my waist. I suspected he was worried I'd bolt and run headlong into the action and my likely demise. His grip hadn't loosened a bit.

"I'm going to shift," I whispered to him over my shoulder, so softly that hopefully none of the shapeshifters would hear me.

He squeezed my waist and froze.

I craned my neck to look behind me. When I met his eyes, his magic rolled and simmered within them once more, like a pair of swirling full moons. For the first time, I wondered how deadly the prince who was so soft on the eyes might be.

"What are you going to shift into?" he asked softly, sounding either incredulous, shocked, or worried. A mixture of all of these emotions, especially the last, was probably appropriate.

I grimaced. "I have no idea." I was just going to hope I wasn't going to *poof* into a guinea pig or a tweety-bird or a tree like Wren.

"I thought you haven't managed a shift before?" he asked, sotto voce.

I smiled, and from the alarm that sped across his face, I guessed I looked as deranged as I felt. "I haven't. But I'm going to now."

If Leander thought Ky was hardheaded, he hadn't

gotten to know me yet. I'd shift by the strength of my will alone to even the odds against my brother.

What did I have to lose? If I failed yet again … no harm done.

But I wouldn't fail.

I couldn't.

18

At first I attempted to summon the blur that preceded every shift I'd witnessed during my time at the academy. Even Dave Bailey's shifts began that way, though it wasn't always immediately recognizable for what it was. But as usual, no blur arrived, and neither did the vibrating and flickering that was supposed to follow that initial stage.

I should've anticipated that despite my determination I wouldn't be able to shift like everyone else did. I'd attempted it too many times. Regardless, there had to be another way available for me, and I couldn't afford to waste another second.

Odds were that I was a shifter of some kind. I had some sort of weird magic to me that no other shifter apparently did. Maybe I could use that to my advantage. Perhaps my neon-glowy goop could spur my transformation. But how? Surely I'd need some notion of how my magic worked to spur anything along, a notion I didn't have and had no clue how to get.

A strained cry arrived from my left and I whipped my head around to where the two mountain lions—and now the quasi—faced off. From the cry, I couldn't tell which of the two lions had been hurt; both were splattered in blood, both surely dipping into their reserves of strength to provide much needed endurance. Their chests labored with heavy breath.

A quick glance at Boone suggested he wasn't faring much better.

I snapped my eyes shut, secure in the fact that Leander wouldn't allow any harm to come to me while I attempted a shift. Let's face it, I was grasping at straws, but when straws were all you had, you hoped like hell you weren't shafted by the short draw.

I leaned my upper body into Leander's chest so I could relax my body. It wasn't at all how Professor McGinty instructed us. I focused on the way my breath swept through me, and the thumping of my heart, which couldn't forget all that was at risk. I focused on *not* noticing how muscled Leander's chest was behind me, or how he'd tightened his hold on me even more after I'd leaned into him. I worked not to breathe in his scent that reminded me of a crisp spring day in the forest, when fragrant flowers were already in bloom. It was no fair; no man should smell this good.

I pushed myself onward.

A pained squeal made me want to open my eyes since I couldn't tell who'd cried out, but I resisted. I squeezed my eyes closed even harder and pushed all my attention toward this energy that ran within me.

The more of my focus I gave to it, the more the energy sparked to life.

My extremities were the first to tingle. They prickled until my hands and feet went numb, my lips and eyeballs almost vibrating from the sensation of it. Then the feeling spread, flowing along the rest of my body like a warm, gushing liquid.

Hmm, it was a pleasant sensation, one I might've confused for arousal for Leander if I hadn't been so intent on ignoring the entirely separate set of tingles his touch sparked within me. The effervescent energy drifted into my abdomen, settling low there.

The energy pooled and began to vibrate, until it made an audible hum. I doubted Leander could hear it, but I certainly could, and it grew loud enough to overshadow the menacing growls and whimpers of the fight.

"Mmm," I murmured, until I realize I was saying it out loud. The realization began to pull me away from where I was sure I needed to be, until I shoved myself back. I'd deal with Leander's reaction to my out-of-place moan later.

My flesh erupted into goose pimples. They circled my skin in a flush. All at once, my flesh burned white hot, but without the pain of combustion. I was hot and cold at once, here and there, in my body and not, probably glowing brightly enough to be spotted by a satellite.

I sucked in a sharp breath as I succumbed to total overload. Overwhelmed by absolutely everything, I was trying to figure out whether I should shut it down before I melted or blew up or something awful, or whether this was what I'd been waiting to happen and should push through.

I hadn't managed to decide by the time I realized that rational thought was nearly beyond me. It was like that moment on a mushroom trip when you first realize the cap was hitting you: I had maybe thirty seconds before I was fruity for Cocoa Puffs.

I didn't think, I didn't try. I reached for the next level, surging my energy outward and hoping that, in doing so, I wasn't messing up Leander. Because at this point I had no real idea what I was doing—none whatsoever. All I knew was that I was experiencing sensations I never had before.

I pictured the energy surging up through my abdomen to the center of my chest, from where it pulsed outward, encompassing every part of me. I shoved and pushed and catapulted outward like I was giving effing birth.

And then something unexpected happened within the already unexpected.

The pulsing picked up speed as if of its own will. As if I'd gifted the energy with its own intelligence, it continued the pattern of swelling energy outward. Much like an electrical surge that would continue so long as power fed it, my energy beat like a drum. Like a heart.

Whatever this was, it was beyond my control. I was spent, using all of my remaining awareness not to black out so that I wouldn't wake to discover myself a melted pile of goo. Because these amounts of energy would do that, I had no doubt. It was like the sun and a nuclear blast folded into one overwhelming package. I couldn't take any more of it. Even with my eyes closed, it was too bright, too much … and I had nowhere to escape what had originated within me.

I crumpled as if I had no bones and no will of my own. Strong, fast arms caught me and swept me off the ground to lean against something hard and warm. A vibration of some sort tried to reach me wherever I was, but against what I'd constructed inside me, it had no chance of reaching me.

Spasms racked my body, making me tense for too long at a time, before giving me a few instants of relief before delivering the next one. I gritted my teeth and squinched my eyes. Every single muscle clenched of its own accord.

Then, just as swiftly as they'd arrived, the spasms ceased, leaving behind a shell that appeared empty the way it sagged and limped in the aftermath of such intensity.

But my vessel was far from empty. It was filled with something greater than me. So much greater.

I arched my back against whatever held me and a final burst of power swept across me. It rolled across my skin, inside and out, like the mother of all tidal waves.

Then it was over. I was spent down to the last drop of blood, the final beat of my heart.

Whatever held me dropped me. I fell … and landed lightly on four feet instead of two.

꧁꧂

IT WOULD HAVE TAKEN A LOT LONGER TO PROCESS
what had happened to me if it hadn't been for the
urgency of the situation and for the fact that I'd actually hoped to shift into some fierce animal capable of
helping my brother and Boone.

As it was, even while the snarls and growls of
animals fighting began to filter through the haze that
had been my consciousness, I struggled to accept that
not only had I accomplished a shift—finally!—but that
I'd transformed into something strong. I wasn't sure
what I was, but my paws were clawed and ample.
When I moved, my muscles glided through my body
like silk. The desire to run free tore through me, and I
had no doubt that if I followed it, I'd run like the wind
on impossibly fast legs.

I shook my head to clear any remaining fog, only
to discover I was already sharp, my senses firing off a
constant stream of input into my brain. I chuffed, and
the sound was a variation of something I'd heard
before ... but what? I struggled to put my finger on it.

I whirled around to seek out Leander, who stood
exactly where I'd left him. The prince stared, silver
eyes wide, and opened and closed his mouth a couple
of times before snapping it shut. A torrent of surprise,
apprehension, and regret swept across his striking face,
making me realize with a start that he'd only allowed
me to attempt a shift because of my stellar track
record of failing at it every time. Of course the protective prince would have intervened if he'd believed I'd

actually morph into an animal and want to charge into battle…

His eyes traveled the length of my body, back and forth, until he finally met my gaze. "Go," he said with evident reluctance. "Help them before it's too late. I'll be right behind you, and I'll get you out if I have to."

Right! My brother. Boone. And an elfin prince who wouldn't hesitate to fly away with me to keep me safe.

I spun in the opposite direction, scanning the animals. Boone and the wolf continued to fight, though it appeared that Boone might have secured the upper hand. With the bear limp on the ground behind them, clinging to the last vestiges of life, my brother was in greater need of assistance. The other wolf's chest heaved with more insistence, his movements more sluggish than Boone's. In the world of animals, even a fractional disadvantage was significant.

I tilted my ears in the direction of my brother before I turned my head toward him. When I did, I discovered that none of the lions were fighting. Three sets of eyes pored over every inch of my body. With the way they stared, I had to remind myself that I wasn't naked. My clothes had vanished along with my magical shift, unlike with the intruders, whose crackling shifts had shredded their clothing.

I was covered in fur, and yet their gazes were too intense; I didn't understand why. Did Ringleader and Quasi understand that this meant the fight was over? That they'd failed in taking us out?

But even Ky was looking at me in the same way they did.

"Let's put an end to this," Leander urged, his tone as succinct as the strike of a lethal weapon.

With the prince right behind me, I stalked toward Ringleader, relishing the way he backed up in careful paces, trying to find the way to keep Ky and myself in his sights at the same time.

Not so fun when the tables are turned, is it? I smiled, unsure what the gesture would look like in this alternate form. With the way Ringleader recoiled at my expression, I imagined my smile actually looked menacing. Good.

I bared my teeth at him, every movement in this body strange and new. But it worked. Ringleader hurried to retreat, and I trailed after him. Ky joined me with continued intermittent looks at Quasi, who appeared even more unsettled by my appearance than his brother.

Ky and I stalked, and Ringleader backed up.

Quasi gave Ky wide berth as he circled around us with skittish looks and fell in behind his brother. Ky growled as he passed, snapping at him, making the deformed animal whimper, jump, and run.

This made Ringleader roar louder than he had during the entire fight, directing the full dose of his fury at Ky. My brother, who'd never been one to do things halfway or to hold back, offered the powerful mountain lion a roar that rivaled his own.

My body hummed with power, eager to respond to Ky's assertion of dominance. I itched to charge and pounce, to sink my teeth into some part of the Ring-leader, who'd invaded the sanctity of our school.

With the threat of Quasi gone, Ky and I merged our approach. Heads low, we stalked our prey.

Ky looked at me and jerked his head a few times, signaling me, I realized. But I didn't read mountain lion. I had no idea what he wanted me to do. He chuffed in exasperation, so familiar in tone that it almost sounded like my human brother, and we continued to stalk the two brothers, who now appeared to intend to escape.

Ringleader flicked a glance at his brother behind him, then spun and sprinted away, back in the direction they'd come. Quasi reacted at the same time his brother did, falling into stride with his retreat—or at least as best as he could given that his gait slowed him.

Ky gave chase while I hesitated. Didn't we want them to leave?

Leander called out to me, "Catch them," he said, so I ran after Ky, reveling in how easy it was to cover the distance, how freeing it was as my speed whipped the breeze past my face and sides.

Ringleader was only a few paces in front of Ky, and my brother was snapping at the heels of Quasi, when that blasted alarm of the school rang out again, causing me to wince at the volume. All four of us animals flinched at the assault until one of the wolves squealed in pain behind us.

I snapped my head around. Leander had stopped shadowing me to stand next to Boone, who had the other wolf pinned to the ground.

I exhaled in relief. Boone was fine.

But by the time I flicked my gaze back to the mountain lions, Ringleader and Quasi were rounding the corner and Ky hovered uncertainly by my side.

He must have accepted the brothers' escape, because he walked up to me to press his nose against mine. The moment he did, I reacted. *The scent of family. Of pride. A lion I could trust. A lion I loved.*

I took in everything about him, learning things about my brother it'd taken me a lifetime in a human body to misunderstand. I'd wanted to shift so desperately that I hadn't realized what the act of it would mean. It was as if my entire perception had changed already, and I'd only been an animal for all of five minutes.

I'd say I wasn't even sure I'd done it right if it weren't for the grace and agility of my movements. There could be no flaw in them.

Ky's copper eyes, a similar color as mine, blazed as they held my own. It was almost as if he were speaking to me.

Then I heard him, deep in the recesses of my mind that had previously only harbored my own thoughts.

'Sister,' he said, 'I'd barely dared to hope.'

I tried to answer, but all I managed was to express thoughts into my own head.

'Mom birthed two mountain lions,' he said. 'I can't believe it.'

I struggled to believe it myself. There was a part of

me that had already realized what I had to be, but the odds were so slim, my hopes too tenuous.

A mountain lion. I tasted the thought and turned it over until I managed to believe it was true and I wasn't dreaming. *A cougar. A puma. A panther.* An animal so majestic it was known by several names.

I followed Ky back to his friends. When I noticed the way Leander was looking at me, the final piece fell into place. I was a mountain lion, and the prince of elves considered me magnificent.

When the blaring siren hushed, a prince, a were-wolf, and a mountain lion snapped their heads in the direction of the gate. My stomach sank as I realized what they must be thinking. Just because the warning had ceased didn't mean the fight was over; it might merely mean that everyone who was expected to arrive in time to make a difference was there.

"Go," Leander said to Boone and Ky. "I'll contain the wolf, secure Rina, and meet you at the gate."

Boone spit the struggling wolf from his mouth; he fell to the ground in a moaning heap and didn't spring up to resume the fight. Leander moved closer, both to the defeated wolf and to me, and Ky and Boone loped off in the direction of the gate.

I hesitated for only a second before running after my brother.

Leander called after me, but I only ran faster. He'd be along soon enough, but who knew how bad the invasion was? If they'd managed to take out the killer rabbit who made me quake in my boots, what kind of threat might they pose to the rest of the staff and students of the Menagerie?

If I could help, I had to. I tried to ignore the question of whether I was forcing Leander to break his promise to my brother as I ran. Certainly the promise had changed now that I was different.

And I was as different as it got. Nothing would ever be the same again.

✢ 19 ✤

I CUT A STRAIGHT LINE ACROSS CAMPUS AND SKIDDED to a stop once the pearly gates came into view. Gone was the angel atop its pillar singing glory through his trumpet. The scary rabbit was still there, but Sir Lancelot had been right. The rabbit would never draw breath again.

I approached the scene slowly, in no hurry now that I saw the immediate danger was over. Sir Lancelot was perched on McGinty's shoulder, but both bird and professor appeared worse for wear, feathers and hair disheveled; a thick spatter of blood marred the leg of McGinty's pants. It could've been from the rabbit or from any of the other bodies strewn across the ground.

The battle here had been more vicious than the one my brother and Boone fought. What looked like the entire staff, minus the vampire professors, who were presumably protecting the fledgling vampires, congregated there. Professor Quickfoot held a battle ax nearly as long as he was tall, coated in bright crimson blood that dripped onto the grass in a steady patter. He crouched over the body of another wolf, newly freed of its head. The gnome's eyes were grave, a sentiment shared by the others there.

None of the advanced students beyond Ky and Boone were present; I guessed they hadn't been needed in the end. From the look of the staff, I could understand why. Every one of them there, even Professor Whittle, the werewolf who taught the most boring version of Beginning Creature History 101 ever, came off as a menace. But the one who was most covered in blood was Marcy June, the ferocious petite female shifter who insisted students dispense with formalities and call her by her given name. She was a teacher of the advanced levels.

She hovered above two of the five felled bodies, clenching and unclenching her fingers as if resisting the urge to tear down a whole army of any who dared invade the school. Her expression remained animalistic, teeth clenched and bared. She must've only just shifted back from whatever animal she became.

A handful of trolls wove through the professors, and though the trolls were entirely nude save for a Tarzan-style loincloth that didn't cover nearly enough, I wouldn't want to mess with them on the best of days. Tar-colored war paint was applied hastily across their faces in streaked lines, making them nothing like the so-ugly-they're-cute Troll Dolls found on eBay. These trolls would beat your ass and probably enjoy it. From the deep scratches across the torso of one, combined with the feral blaze that streaked his beady black eyes, and the blood droplets that spotted every one of them, they'd been in the middle of the brawl.

I'd permanently be on my best behavior in the dining hall, from now until like … ever.

Then my gaze returned to the rabbit and a wave of pity swirled through me. Though he'd been the most terrifying thing I'd ever seen—well, maybe along with the trolls and that Marcy June who was snarling like she was disappointed she didn't have more shifters to kill—the rabbit had died defending the school and every creature within it.

And he'd fought hard. From the looks of things, he'd been taken down by overwhelming force. His tall frame was as much red as it was brown, his thick fur interrupted everywhere by wide, gaping gashes. Fur was ripped and peeled back, his long black pants and button-down shirt torn and shredded. An entire ear was shorn from his head.

The rabbit had died with a sneer on his face, eyes open wide, glaring at his enemy, both large, floppy feet bent in unnatural directions, suggesting his body had been broken as well as torn. The determined expression on his face promised they'd only managed to break his body, not his will—not his resolve in fulfilling his oath to protect the Magical Creatures Academy until his final breath.

The heavy, mournful breaths of those gathered were louder than they should be to my ears. For the loss wasn't just for one of our own, it was for the sanctity of all that the school represented, here nestled deep inside the safety of a magical mountain. Before now, the Menagerie had been considered impregnable. That myth had been dispelled in the most violent of fashions.

The blue spring sky suddenly seemed less bright, the chirping of birds out of place and somehow wrong. Whatever was coming next wouldn't belong in this idyllic atmosphere Thunder Mountain harbored. These shifters who'd attacked had declared war.

Ringleader and Quasi had escaped. And here, from the bloodied state of the staff, I guessed the fight had involved more than the numbers pooled dead on the ground. With the keen vision and scent of my lion, I marked trails of blood leading away from the scene. There'd been many more who'd attacked.

Sir Lancelot's big yellow eyes were clouded. The owl, who appeared always to have something to say, pursed his beak shut as he surveyed the damage. He shook his head, the ruffled feathers atop his crown flopping with his movements.

Until his eyes landed on me. Fast as a flash, they flicked to Ky then back to me. His eyes widened and his beak dropped open.

Seconds thumped by. "Rina?" he finally asked.

I nodded as every creature there followed the owl's attention.

"Ky's sister?" Marcy June asked.

"Yes," Professor McGinty said, the one word dragged out with awe.

Shocked silence tried to take hold until McGinty barked with laughter. He slapped his thigh on the opposite side of Sir Lancelot. "How about that, lassie? You shifted after all. And you're a friggin' mountain lion!" His voice grew louder. "A mountain lion!"

The headmaster owl winced.

"What do you think of that, Ky?" the shifter professor continued as if Ky weren't in the body of an animal and we weren't standing around the scene of a massacre. McGinty hooted. The trolls scowled, though at what exactly, who knew; it was their favorite expression.

"That means she's a dual mage shifter," Sir Lancelot whispered, and though his voice was soft, his words sliced through me to the core. Ky's muscles twitched as he startled. "Or something," the owl continued. "I don't think it's ever occurred before. There isn't even a name for it."

Wait, I wanted to say. *We still don't know for sure that my glowy goop is the power of mages.* But I couldn't say a thing. I was a mountain lion.

I was an effing lion! Now that the immediate threat of death had abated, the fact tried to take root within me. I struggled to absorb how my reality had changed. Denial had its grip on me no matter what evidence surrounded me.

Everyone was staring at me and their attention was cutting through to my very nerves. I twitched with the urge to swat their gazes away with a flick of my tail.

When footsteps sounded behind us, I turned, grateful for the distraction. It was Leander, and he was dragging a naked man who looked like he was lucky to be alive. Cuts bled freely across his body, but his throat bled the most of all. I was amazed the man was able to stand upright despite the blood loss, then I remembered shifters had extraordinarily fast healing—which was why to kill them one had to inflict mortal wounds from which they'd have no chance to recover.

"Who is this you bring, Leander?" Sir Lancelot's voice rang out across the grass dotted with flowers.

Leander's eyes found me before he answered. When he spotted me, an edge fled his eyes, their silver gray settling from a boil to a simmer. "A wolf Boone incapacitated. He's a member of the Voice."

"I see," Sir Lancelot said. "I take this to mean you were also attacked?"

The prince nodded. "We were. By four shifters, as soon as we exited Bundry Hall."

A few gasps of outrage came from the professors, while McGinty and Sir Lancelot's faces settled into similar lines of disgust.

"Boone killed one, a bear, who's now entirely relieved of his life force. The two Ky fought ran away."

"The cowards," McGinty spat.

Marcy June growled in agreement, sounding more like an animal than a woman. "Chicken shits," she said in a tone that was several octaves too low for her petite frame.

Leander nodded again. "One of those Ky fought, the largest of the shifters there, was also a mountain lion."

"W-what?" Professor Whittle asked.

"Yes, a mountain lion, and a fine specimen of one. The second was similar to a mountain lion, but off."

"As if he didn't quite possess the strength of magic to fully embody the mountain lion?" Sir Lancelot asked.

"Exactly like that. He was deformed, if he was a mountain lion at all."

Sir Lancelot and Professor Whittle exchanged a weighted glance.

"You can't mean it's Rage and Fury?" McGinty asked, head tilted to address the owl on his shoulder.

"The shifter here is quite chatty when properly motivated," Leander said, before Sir Lancelot had the chance to answer.

Leander gave the naked wolf man a firm tug and shoved him into the center of our haphazard circle. The shifter tripped and stumbled, then froze surveying the bodies that littered the ground around him.

The threat was tacit and the wolf man was sharp enough to get it: he'd be next if he didn't answer any questions asked of him.

"Were these shifters Rage and Fury?" Sir Lancelot asked of the wolf man, who scanned our circle, finally landing on me and resting there for a few seconds too many, his eyes jumpy.

"Answer the headmaster's question," McGinty growled in menace, and Professor Quickfoot stepped around a few bodies and into the center of the circle, swinging his bloody ax.

Wolf Man's eyes widened and tittered. When Marcy June moved to Quickfoot's other side, curling her fingers as if she'd tear into him with her bare hands, he rushed to answer. "Rage and Fury, yeah."

McGinty whistled. "The infamous mountain lion brothers."

Ky and I flicked our heads toward the shifter professor. Mountain lion brothers? I'd thought there were only two mountain lion shifters in the entire world now that Mom was dead. Three including me now.

Ky's lion blurred, vibrated, and flickered so quickly that everyone waited for him to shift before continuing with the questioning. When he settled back into his uniform, blood immediately soaked through his shirt and pant leg. Still, his injuries were none that Melinda, and his shifter magic, wouldn't be able to resolve.

He stalked toward Wolf Man while Boone instigated his own shift. "What do you mean? Who are these brothers?" Ky looked between the enemy and Sir Lancelot, McGinty, and Whittle.

Wolf Man laughed, a raucous, strident giggle that would've been well suited to a madhouse. "The brothers who are going to devour you or this sweet fresh mountain lion." He chuckled and it sent shivers through my body all the way down to my paws. "Better yet, Rage'll probably take you both."

"What's this asshole talking about?" Ky asked Sir Lancelot. It was a sign of his anger that he'd curse in front of the well-mannered owl.

Boone, now back to being human, and Leander, stepped into the middle of the rough circle, joining Ky.

"Rage is a powerful shifter," Whittle said. "One of the strongest. He and his brother, Fury, were born less than a year apart from each other. They were both mountain lions, something unheard of in the shifter world."

For once the ancient werewolf's lesson intrigued me. I hung on his every word, moving closer to him before realizing it.

"They rose in ranks of the rebel shifters quickly, outpowering many of the other shifters, both as animals and humans. Rumors tell they're ruthless."

"Yeah, they're going to come for these young lions and butcher them," Wolf Man sneered. Marcy June lunged at him, putting all her anger into a jump and ripping into his jaw with a bone-crunching uppercut.

Wolf Man crumpled to the ground, where he didn't move or make a peep. She'd knocked him out cold.

Quickfoot rested a boot and the head of his ax atop the shifter, where the ax smeared blood against the shifter's bare chest. I'd never be able to look at the professor the same way again. I'd actually considered the gnome with his red hat and grandfather-like eyes cute and gentle at one point. How wrong I'd been.

The trolls edged around the fallen werewolf, and I hoped like hell they weren't about to tear into the guy while he was unconscious. From the way their war paint crinkled around vicious sneers, I wasn't sure they wouldn't.

"Continue, Wendell," Sir Lancelot said.

Professor Whittle did, in a tremulous voice. "Rage

and Fury were in a car accident that would've certainly killed them if not for their shifter healing."

"But they were horribly injured," McGinty continued, "though now I'm certain they deserved what they got."

Whittle nodded absently. "It would seem. Rage was injured worst of all, so badly that he lost his shifter power entirely at the end and would have certainly died."

"He should've," Marcy June snarled, to the agreement of several of the other professors, including McGinty and Quickfoot.

"Without his shifter healing, Rage's injuries overcame him. Non-magical interventions had no chance of saving him," Whittle said. "So Fury sacrificed his shifter power to save his brother. Enlisting the help of a very dark sorcerer, Fury managed to gift his brother with enough of his shifter power to allow Rage to recover. Fury, however, lost almost all of his mountain lion. It's rumored that when he shifts, he's nothing but a deformed shell of his former creature."

"That would explain what we saw," Ky said. "I couldn't figure out what the animal was."

Boone nodded.

Sir Lancelot appeared to be deep in thought when he snapped his head up and stared straight at me, eyes blazing as they burrowed into me. "Did Fury and Rage see Rina?"

"They did," Ky said.

The owl squeaked. "Then that means this fallen

werewolf was right. Rage will come after Rina and Ky, Rina especially."

"Why Rina?" Ky asked, as if the strength of his conviction alone could protect me. "Why not just me?"

"Because Rage has been searching for the way to replenish his brother's shifter power," Whittle said in that slow monotone voice of his. "Ever since the accident, he's rumored to have worked with this dark sorcerer seeking the way. I believe the only way will be to steal the power from another shifter of the same kind." Whittle looked to the owl for verification.

"That is my understanding too, Wendell." That wasn't good news. The owl was rumored to know almost everything. To Ky, he said, "He might come after you as well as Rina, figuring either of the two of you would suit his purposes. But if he figures out that Rina has mage powers as well as those of a shifter ... well, what do you think a power-hungry shifter like him will do?"

No one needed to say a word. We all knew the answer to that question.

If only I hadn't shifted in front of them ... but then maybe Ky or Boone would have died along with Rasper the Rabbit.

As it was, I'd offered myself up to the only other mountain lion shifters in the world. On a tidy platter.

20

THE WEEKS UNTIL THE END OF TERM DRAGGED OUT, AS much because of the tension that now permeated every aspect of campus life as because I was already worried about what would happen once school let out. Individually, Ky and I were on the Voice's most wanted list, since apparently Rage was the head of the shifter rebels represented by the group. Fury was his close second, lesser in rank only because he currently lacked the power that shifters respected.

Together, Ky and I had a big-ass neon target painted across our backs. The smart thing would've been for us to split up, I supposed, to separate the treasure no doubt Rage sought. But Ky and I were scheduled to return home at the end of May, where there'd be no one around to protect us but Dad.

Just the thought of Dad and how much he'd lost already made my stomach roil. How would he react once he learned the only family he had left was in imminent danger? I nibbled at my cuticles since I'd already chewed my nails down to stubs.

"You're worrying again," Wren said. Her voice had been laced with concern for me since the Attack —with a capital "A"—as everyone was referring to it.

"How could she not worry?" Dave Bailey said from where we sat on the grass to soak up the sunshine. It helped to dispel the sense of doom that had circled the school like an infectious disease. "Those shifters are effing insane."

Jas slapped him on the shoulder.

"Hey! What was that for?"

"Because you have to learn a little tact. You can't just blurt things out like that. Can't you see she's already freaked out from worrying so much?"

Wren and I exchanged a lighthearted glance that said, *Is she serious?* Talk about the pot calling the kettle black. I welcomed the amusement; I'd found too little of it as of late, and I was desperate for something to distract from my likely death.

"Obviously she has reason to worry," Jas continued. "She's being hunted by Rage *and* Fury, for fuck's sake. Their names alone are enough to make most people shit their pants." She paused, I hoped to get a sense for how unhelpful what she was saying was. "I mean, who knows what they might do to her if they get their hands on her?"

Nope. No reflection at all.

Jas shook her head, causing the thick white streak to slide across her forehead and set the gem in her nose ring to swinging. "They need her mountain lion shifter magic, but they won't need her alive after they take it."

"Jas!" Wren admonished.

When Jas looked up at our soft-spoken friend, she genuinely didn't seem to understand what she'd done wrong. Too fast, her plucked eyebrows settled back down across her forehead and she continued speaking. "I can't believe Ky is under threat too. He's too hot for the threat of death. Hmm, though it kind of amplifies his bad boy persona, doesn't it? It makes him all dangerous-like."

I didn't know where to start taking offense. Should it be with how she sounded like she cared more about my brother than me, even though they'd barely exchanged words over the length of the term?

"What are you going to be doing over the summer, Dave?" Wren asked to change the subject before I could strangle Jas.

"My parents want to travel this summer, so we'll be going to Europe—I think that's what they said."

Europe sounded good. Great, really. Being on a different continent than the shifter brothers seemed like a fine idea.

Dave shrugged with an apologetic look at me. "I think they also want to get away from here for a while. They've been really worried since the Attack. They've been sending Talk-a-Letters almost non-stop since it happened." He rolled his eyes. "It's been so embarrassing."

I half-smiled. "Hey, at least you've gotten your shifts down now, right? That's awesome."

He grinned. "So awesome. I can't wait until next term when I can take it to the next level."

Jas snorted. "You mean the kindergarten level?" She laughed at her own joke. After realizing none of us was laughing with her, she said, "It's a joke, guys. I'm saying he was a pre-schooler this year, get it?"

"Jasmine Jolly," Wren said in her most severe tone. "You have an acute case of foot-in-mouth. Girl, you need to learn to just shut it sometimes. We're your friends, not your punching bags."

My mouth dropped open. "Whoa, Wren. Where've you been hiding this side of yourself?"

She smiled and adjusted her shoulders. "I've always been sassy."

Dave was eyeing her in a way I'd never noticed him eyeing her before. "Well, I like this side of you. You should speak your mind more often." He pointed a hooked thumb over at Jas. "She should speak it less."

But Jas had her eyes narrowed at Wren. With how thick her mascara and eyeliner were, and how bright the blue of her eyes, the look was unsettling, especially when you factored in the low growl rumbling through her chest. "You called me 'Jasmine,' and you even called me 'Jolly.'"

"It's your name. Deal with it." Wren wasn't cowering, and I took in my roommate as if for the first time. Dave was right, this side of her suited her quite well. She'd left the persona of the drooping willow tree far behind.

Jas growled, louder this time.

"Look, here comes Adalia," Dave said with a

panicked glance at me. Jas sounded like she was about to tackle Wren to the ground. If she did, there was no way Wren would win. Jas was a brawler, and Wren was too sweet, no matter how much sass she released.

His distraction should have worked, given how much Jas claimed to despise the upbeat fairy, but Jas didn't move her focus from Wren.

"She looks happier than usual," Dave added.

That did it. Jas snapped her head around to take in the beautiful fairy bouncing across the grass to join us. Nancy, the academy's staff witch, had erased all traces of blood and gore from the campus. The only signs that the Attack had taken place at all were the nagging memories I couldn't shake no matter how hard I tried.

"Hey, guys," Adalia called ahead with a beaming smile across her pretty face.

Dave, Wren, and I waved and smiled back. Jas crossed her arms and sulked. "Why won't she leave me the eff alone?"

"Maybe it's your sparkling personality," Dave said with a mischievous grin that reminded me of why I liked the awkward guy as much as I did.

"Must be," Jas growled, as Adalia lowered herself onto the grass close to Jas, plopping a small pile of books next to her. The fairy was either the smartest or the stupidest person I'd ever met; I'd been trying to decide all semester without luck.

"Hey there, roomie," Adalia said to Jas. "It's a beautiful day, isn't it?"

Jas grunted.

"I can't believe we're going to be heading home soon. I'm going to miss this place."

"Me too," I said, and Wren patted me on the back in sympathy. "I'll even miss the trolls, and I never in a million years thought I'd say that."

"The trolls are great," Adalia said. "I love the flair to their hair. They're so cute."

Jas snorted and Adalia winked at me. I narrowed my eyes at her.

"It makes me happy just to look at them," she said.

Jas threw her hands in the air while she muttered something unintelligible, undoubtedly sparing our ears from cursing that would've made a hardened sailor proud.

Adalia grinned at me when Jas wasn't looking, too disgusted by the sight of the happy fairy to look at her.

My mouth dropped open. Adalia had been playing Jas all this time! Months of this, and it turned out she was one of the slickest creatures on campus. Wow. I couldn't wait to talk to Wren about it later. Go Adalia. She'd beat Jas at her own game. Brilliant.

When I finally grinned at Adalia, she grinned right back, her opalescent eyes sparkling with what I now readily identified as mischief.

"When do you leave for the Forest?" Wren asked Adalia. Everyone but Dave was returning home. Wren was going back to her large hippie family, and Jas was spending the summer with her parents at their Upstate New York estate. Her parents were rich and she was an only child. Go figure.

"Oh, as soon as the prince is ready to go," Adalia

said. "All the fae will be traveling back together, since Prince Leander Verion will be opening a portal for all of us. He said he'll be ready whenever Rina is."

"Me? Why would he be ready when I am?"

"You're going with us. Didn't anybody tell you?"

"No, nobody told me anything. What are you talking about?"

"Well," Adalia said, "since the Voice is hunting you and Ky, Sir Lancelot and Prince Leander Verion figured you'd be safest in the land of the fae, since nobody can go there without permission from the fae."

"Kind of how no one's allowed to enter the Menagerie without permission?" Jas muttered and I hurried to ignore her before I could think of any additional reason to fret.

"The king of the elves has already agreed to it," Adalia said. "And the king is powerful. It's the best place for you, especially since your shifter powers are unstable."

No kidding. I'd been stuck in the body of a mountain lion for nearly a week after my shift, until I figured out how to return myself to my human form. Despite my dedication and McGinty's constant encouragement, my shifts hadn't achieved stability or consistency. It was still a crap shoot every time I considered turning into a lion. I hadn't had any Dave Bailey shifts where my two shapes merged in a mess of body parts, but I wasn't too far off. I only managed to shift maybe a third of the time, and then there was no guarantee I'd be able to shift back in a timely manner.

LUCÍA ASHTA

On top of that, my glowy goop magic hadn't made a return appearance, frustrating Sir Lancelot until he was speechless. He'd been hoping to more closely study my magic to determine whether or not I was indeed a dual shifter-mage as he suspected.

"Why would the king agree to have me there?" I asked. "My powers are super unstable *and* I have a bulls-eye on my head."

"Prince Leander Verion can be very persuasive." She gave me a knowing smile and I blushed, though I wasn't sure I believed what I thought she was implying. "And Ky is one of his best friends besides. Ky'd do the same thing for the prince if the roles were reversed."

"Yeah, I imagine he would."

"It's too bad the Enforcers can't help protect you," Dave said, and for once not even Jas had a snarky remark to offer. The Attack had come only after the Voice had invaded the Enforcers' headquarters. They'd gone in the middle of the night, when the vampire faction of the Voice could bolster their forces, and killed the majority of the Enforcers while they slept.

The invasion had been unexpected. The Voice had done nothing to suggest such underhanded actions. Their public announcement of their desire for the Enforcers to stop policing them hadn't suggested what would happen if the Enforcers didn't heed their demands. Certainly no one had expected them to behave with such a blatant lack of honor. The entire magical community was reeling from the Voice's actions.

Many of those who'd been sympathetic to the Voice's desire for autonomy before had since done everything they could to separate themselves from their actions. A firm line divided the factions now: those who wanted freedom to do as they wished both in the magical and non-magical circles at any cost, and those who believed everyone blessed with magic should stick together. Even weeks after the Voice wiped out most of the Enforcers, outrage was loud among the magical community at the Voice's violation of basic codes of honor and humanity.

The Enforcers, who'd numbered nearly seven hundred, remained in no more than handfuls. The bare bones of the organization struggled to fulfill its role when the dangers to police were greater than ever before.

"I still can't believe it," Wren said, her eyes growing misty.

Though neither my friends nor I had known any Enforcers personally, we'd all cried at their violent deaths. Even Jas had smeared her eyeliner and mascara and cursed up a storm at the injustice.

"To think they'd all graduated from this same school," Dave said. "They were all just like us at one time."

"I don't think anyone's exactly like us," Jas said. "We're as unique as they come. Especially you and your quirky-ass self."

But none of us chuckled at her lame attempt at a

joke, not even her. We sat in the silence of mourning until Jas started primping. Her skirt was shorter than the allowed mid-thigh length, and two of the top buttons of her shirt were unbuttoned instead of the permitted one. She made sure her skirt revealed most of a thigh and tucked her hair behind her ears.

I looked across the quad to see my brother approaching. Leander and Boone were with him.

Adalia rose to her feet and tugged her skirt down, the opposite direction as Jas. When Leander was within earshot, she bowed deeply. "My Prince," she said.

Leander offered her a regal smile before looking at me. His mercurial gaze revealed something different than usual, but what?

Ky crouched next to me and Jas scooted closer to us. I didn't bother glaring at her; I'd tired of doing it, as she'd worked all semester to gain my brother's attention. If only she realized that my brother was far too preoccupied to consider it; he'd been in big-brother protector mode since the Attack.

"Leander has invited us to stay with him during the summer," Ky said. "It's a very kind offer since his father has agreed to extend the protection of his crown while we're there."

I met Leander's glimmering eyes. "Thank you."

"It's my pleasure." And though his voice was regal, the choice of words made a thrill run through me that should've had no place in bleak times like this. Leander could definitely deliver pleasure.

Guilt swept across my face at the thought, and

when his eyes sparked, I flushed as if he'd truly read my mind.

I hurriedly tucked my face behind Ky. Boy, I was in trouble if I had to spend the summer with the prince and I couldn't behave any better than this. *Life and death, Rina. Life and death.* Still, I was pretty sure my heart—or maybe I could blame my hormones—didn't give a damn.

"What do you say?" Ky asked.

"I think it's a good idea. We can't go home to Dad like this."

"I'd rather not."

"Do you think he'll be okay without us?"

Ky shrugged, but the gesture only faked nonchalance. "He'll do better without us than with the danger we'd bring."

I nodded, also trying to convince myself we had to do this. Dad hadn't been home alone without one of us there since Mom died giving birth to me. Now Ky and I'd been gone all term and we were only going to extend that until, when, winter vacation next year? That was a long time for Dad, but what else could we do?

"I'll be going too," Boone said, and Wren turned wistful eyes on the ruggedly handsome werewolf. "My father has decided those of us wolves who are honorable have a stake in all this. He wants me to keep a close eye on the situation, and since you two are at the center of it all, he wants me near you."

"Sounds good," I said. Boone was strong, capable, and I liked him. And it'd be one more person as a guest of the fae to help me feel less awkward about it. "So when do we leave?" I asked.

"As soon as you're ready," Ky said. "We've already been dismissed from course requirements."

"Okay. So Friday after my last class?"

"That was what we'd thought, but Sir Lancelot thinks it'd be better if we go now."

"Now?" I squeaked with a panicked look at the too-beautiful elfin prince.

"Sir Lancelot thinks the Voice might be watching for your departure," Boone said. "I think he's right. It's what I'd do. We need to catch them off guard so they don't attack while Leander creates the portal for us."

"Can't he just do it here?" I cleared my throat to try to keep my voice from squeaking.

"I can't," Leander said. "The mountain is protected against portals, one of the many security measures in place."

I swallowed my bitterness that the protection measures hadn't been enough. The shifters had muscled their way through the school's guardian rabbit, and that was all it'd taken to give them full access to the campus.

"I'd like to leave right now," Leander continued.

"W-what about clothes or any of my stuff?" The truth was that I had very few personal belongings here; he'd know it too. None of us brought much since the school provided nearly everything we needed.

"I'll make sure you have everything you need in

the Forest," he said while his eyes suggested that "everything" might include more than physical items.

I was nodding and standing before I realized what I was doing. I couldn't say no to the prince, not when his actions were guided by thoughts of my well-being. "What about my coursework? I'm still not finished."

"Sir Lancelot has cleared everything," Ky said. "Besides, you don't do much of anything the last few days. Even the teachers are thinking of vacation."

It was certainly like that at Berry Bramble High too, which seemed like a lifetime ago.

"Okay, then … I guess." I sounded as uncertain as I felt. "Get up and give me hugs, guys."

Wren, Dave, and Adalia popped right up. Jas followed last. My friends hugged me like we'd never see each other again. I hoped with all my heart that wasn't the case.

"I'll see you soon," Adalia whispered, and it helped. At least I'd have one friend there besides my brother.

I blinked back tears and faced off with Leander.

"Are you ready?" he said, and from the way he said it I was sure he meant was I ready for him.

When I answered, "I sure as hell hope so," I meant it in every sense of the word.

I followed the prince to the edge of campus without turning back. When we crossed the pearly gates, I didn't look down once at the patch of grass that contained so many awful memories.

I trailed behind Leander's strong shoulders, determined to put the past behind me and to embrace all the potential of my future. Magic brewed inside me, and I was ready to embrace all it delivered. I wasn't returning to Iowa. I was going to the fae's Golden Forest.

Life was preparing to deliver amazing magical experiences and I didn't mind in the least that they were going to contain Leander Verion, prince of the elves, in a starring role. I'd trail his fine ass anywhere he wanted to take me.

As if he felt my gaze searing into his body, he turned to look at me over his shoulder. He winked those sparkling silver eyes of his.

What the hell? I winked back and grinned. After the term I'd survived, I deserved to have a little fun. Prince of the elves, bring it on.

LION SHIFTER

Magical Creatures Academy: **Book Two**

Continue Rina's adventures in *Lion Shifter*!

ACKNOWLEDGMENTS

I'd write no matter what, because telling stories is a passion, but the following people make creating worlds (and life) a joy. I'm eternally grateful for the support of my beloved, James, my mother, Elsa, and my three daughters, Catia, Sonia, and Nadia. They've always believed in me, even before I published a single word. They help me see the magic in the world around me, and more importantly, within.

I'm thankful for every single one of you who've reached out to tell me that one of my stories touched you in one way or another, made you smile or cry, or kept you up long past your bedtime. You've given me reason to keep writing.

ABOUT THE AUTHOR

Lucía Ashta is the Amazon top 100 bestselling author of young adult and new adult paranormal and urban fantasy books, including the series *Magical Creatures Academy*, *Sirangel*, *Magical Arts Academy*, *Witching World*, *Dragon Force*, and *Supernatural Bounty Hunter*.

When Lucía isn't writing, she's reading, painting, or adventuring. Magical fantasy is her favorite, but the action, romance, and quirky characters are what keep her hooked on books.

A former attorney and architect, she's an Argentinian-American author who lives in Sedona with her beloved and three daughters. She published her first story (about an unusual Cockatoo) at the age of eight, and she's been at it ever since.